beetle® bailey

GENERAL ALERT

by
mort walker

TOR

A TOM DOHERTY ASSOCIATES BOOK
NEW YORK

This is a work of fiction. All the characters and events portrayed in this book are fictitious, and any resemblance to real people or events is purely coincidental.

BEETLE BAILEY: GENERAL ALERT

The cartoons in this book also appeared in the Giant Size BEETLE BAILEY: GENERAL ALERT

A Tor Book
Published by Tom Doherty Associates, Inc.
49 West 24th Street
New York, N.Y. 10010

ISBN: 0-812-51506-4

Printed in the United States of America

0 9 8 7 6 5 4 3 2 1

Don't miss these other Beetle Bailey titles published by Tor Books!

BEETLE BAILEY: ADVANCED PLANNING
BEETLE BAILEY: DOUBLE TROUBLE
BEETLE BAILEY: A FLYING BEETLE?
BEETLE BAILEY: HEY THERE!
BEETLE BAILEY: NOT REVERSE
BEETLE BAILEY: POTATO FANCAKES!
BEETLE BAILEY: QUIT CLOWNING AROUND
BEETLE BAILEY: REVENGE
BEETLE BAILEY: THE ROUGH RIDERS
BEETLE BAILEY: SARGE IS A DOPE!
BEETLE BAILEY: SEPARATE CHECKS
BEETLE BAILEY: SURPRISE PACKAGE
BEETLE BAILEY: TAKE TEN
BEETLE BAILEY: THAT SINKING FEELING
BEETLE BAILEY: THREE'S A CROWD
BEETLE BAILEY: TOUGH LUCK
BEETLE BAILEY: UNCLE SAM WANTS YOU
BEETLE BAILEY: UNDERCOVER OPERATION
BEETLE BAILEY: WELCOME TO CAMP SWAMPY!
BEETLE BAILEY: YOU CRACK ME UP

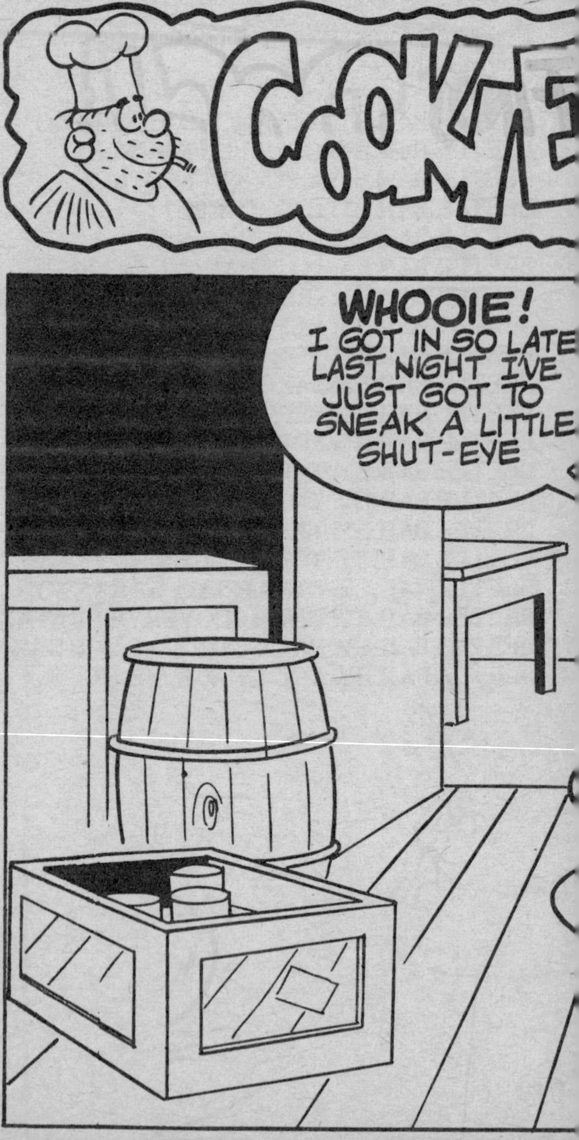
COOKIE
WHOOIE! I GOT IN SO LATE LAST NIGHT I'VE JUST GOT TO SNEAK A LITTLE SHUT-EYE

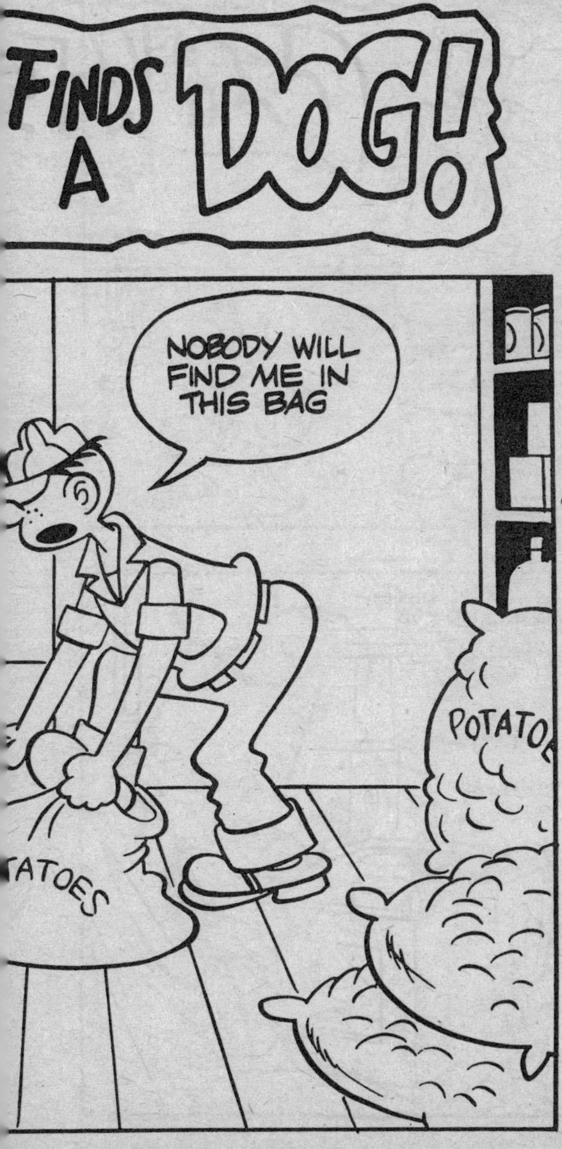
FINDS A DOG!
NOBODY WILL FIND ME IN THIS BAG
POTATO
TATOES

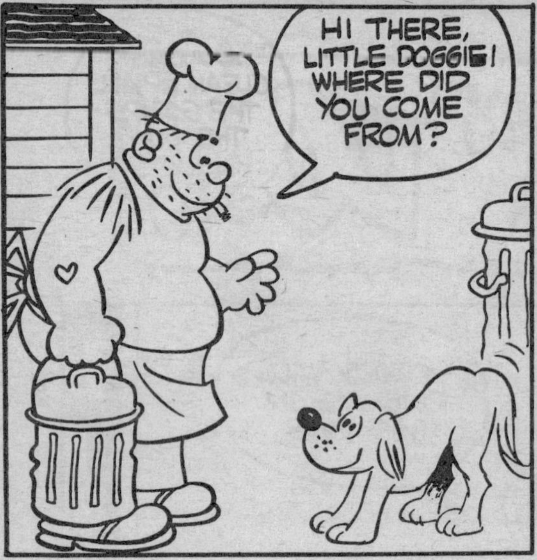
HI THERE, LITTLE DOGGIE! WHERE DID YOU COME FROM?

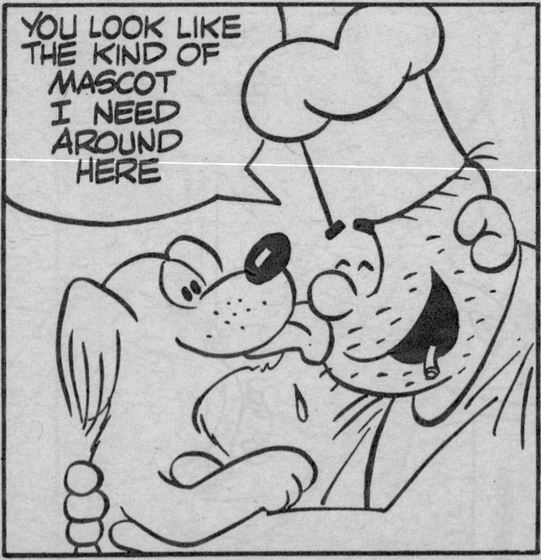
YOU LOOK LIKE THE KIND OF MASCOT I NEED AROUND HERE

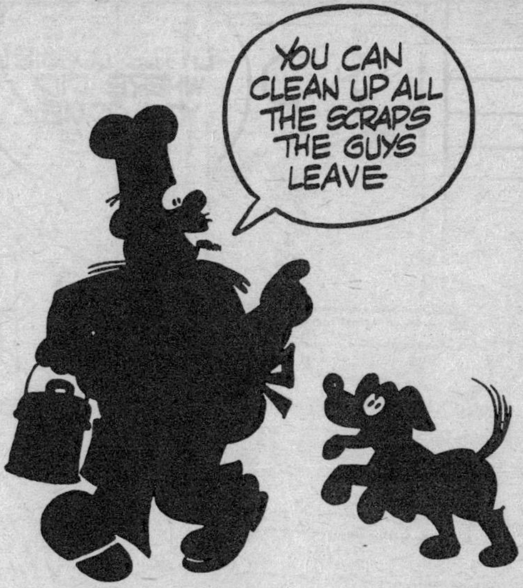
YOU CAN CLEAN UP ALL THE SCRAPS THE GUYS LEAVE

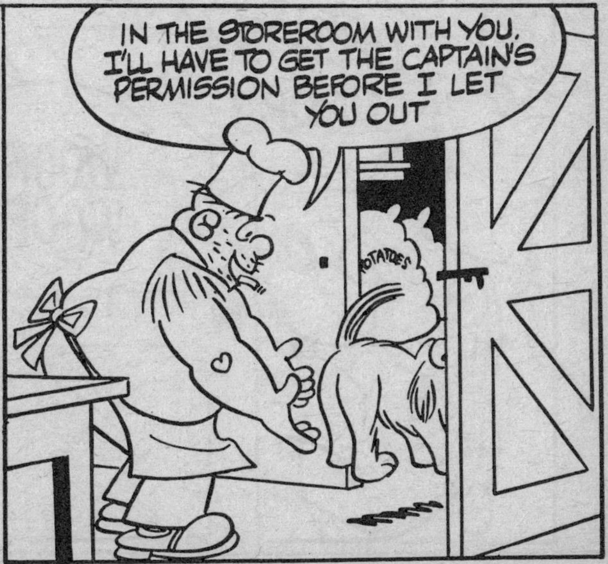
IN THE STOREROOM WITH YOU. I'LL HAVE TO GET THE CAPTAIN'S PERMISSION BEFORE I LET YOU OUT
POTATOES

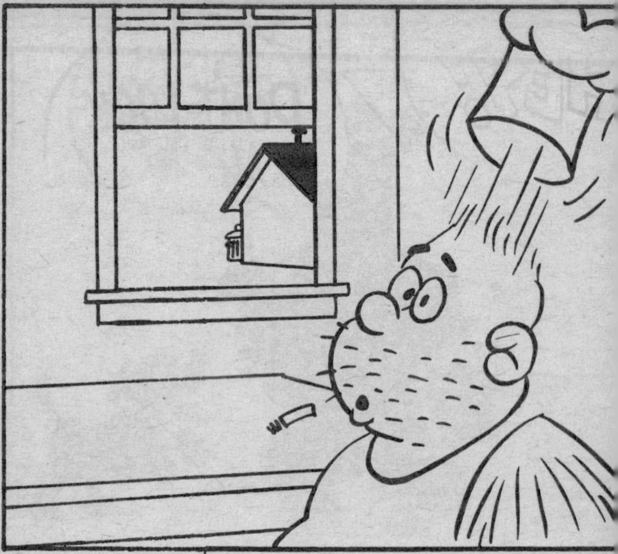

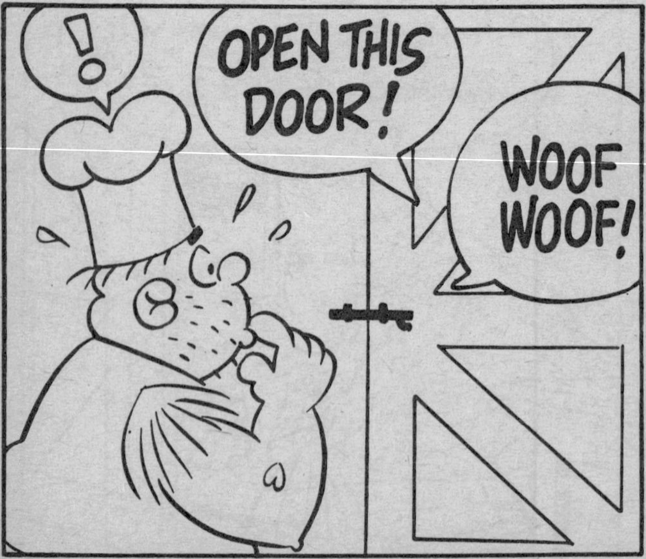
!
OPEN THIS DOOR!
WOOF WOOF!

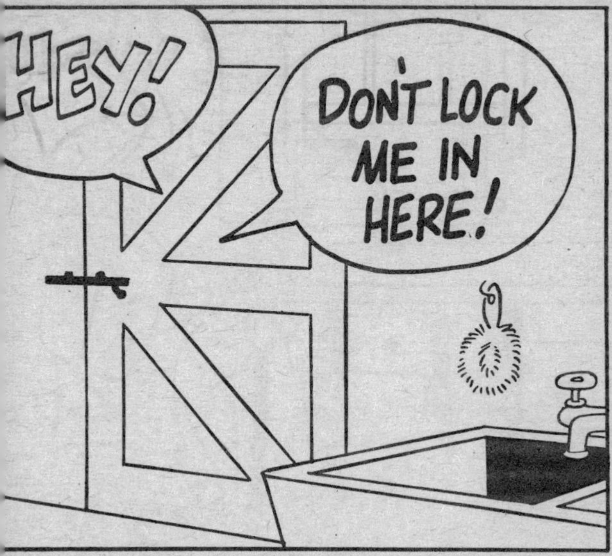
HEY!
DON'T LOCK ME IN HERE!

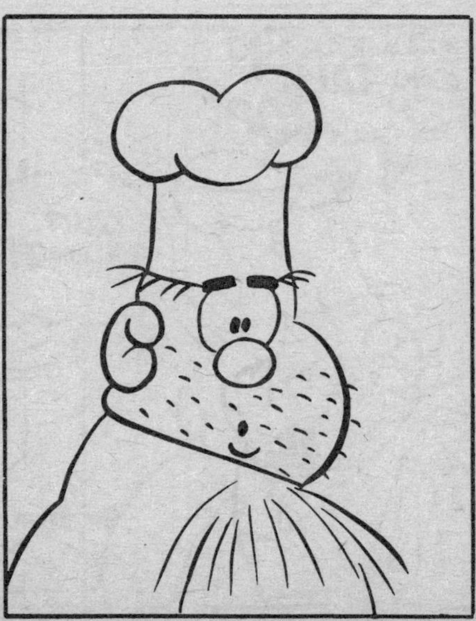

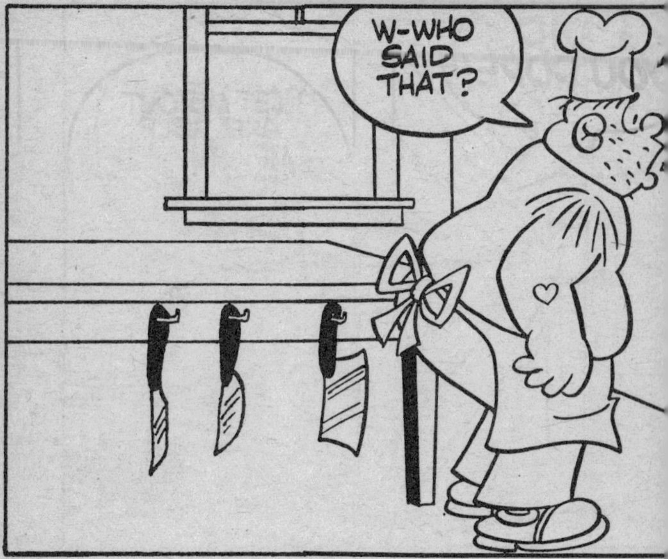
W-WHO SAID THAT?

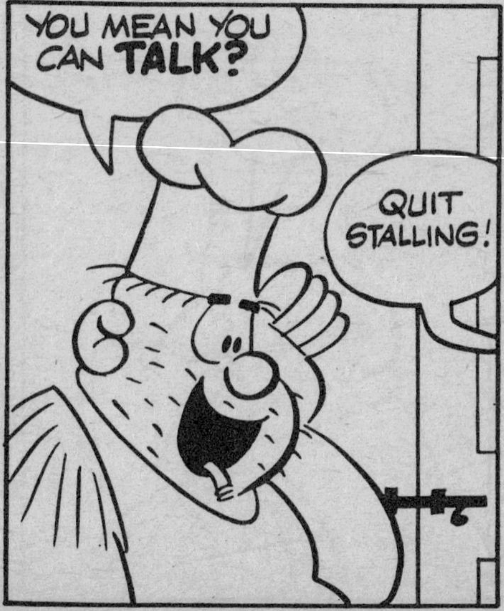
YOU MEAN YOU CAN **TALK**?
QUIT STALLING!

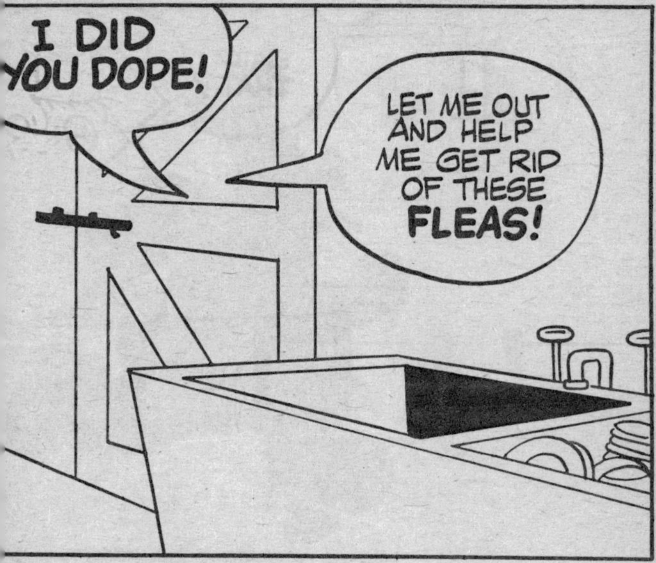
I DID YOU DOPE!
LET ME OUT AND HELP ME GET RID OF THESE **FLEAS!**

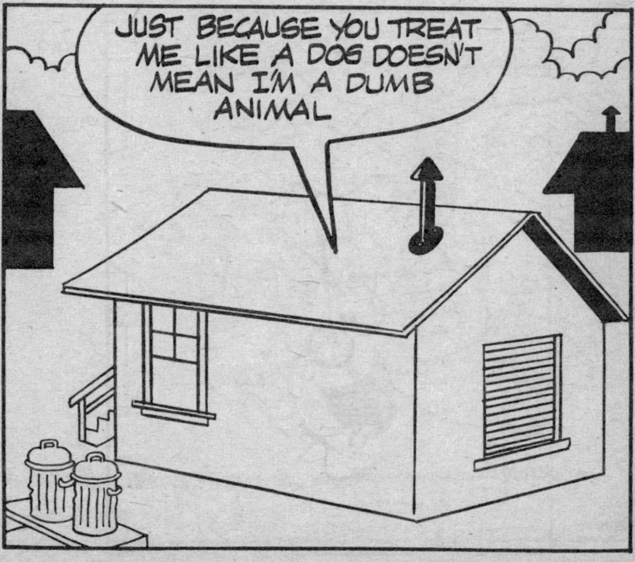
JUST BECAUSE YOU TREAT ME LIKE A DOG DOESN'T MEAN I'M A DUMB ANIMAL

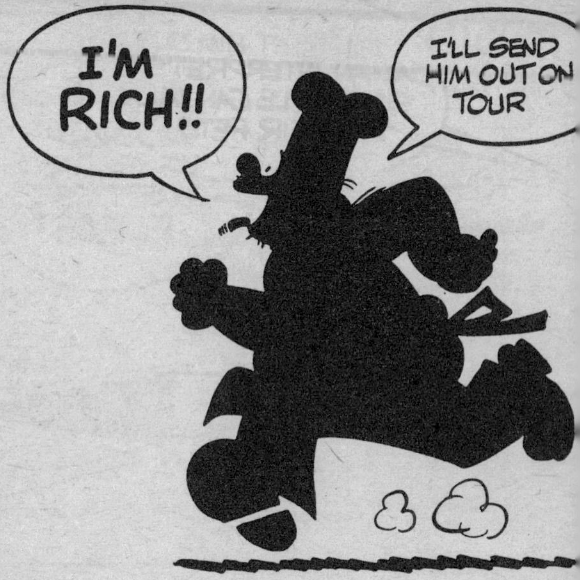
I'M RICH!!
I'LL SEND HIM OUT ON TOUR

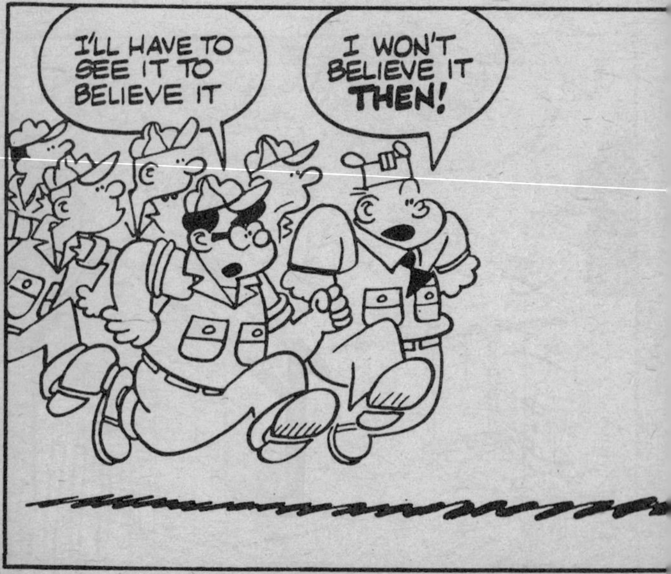
I'LL HAVE TO SEE IT TO BELIEVE IT
I WON'T BELIEVE IT THEN!

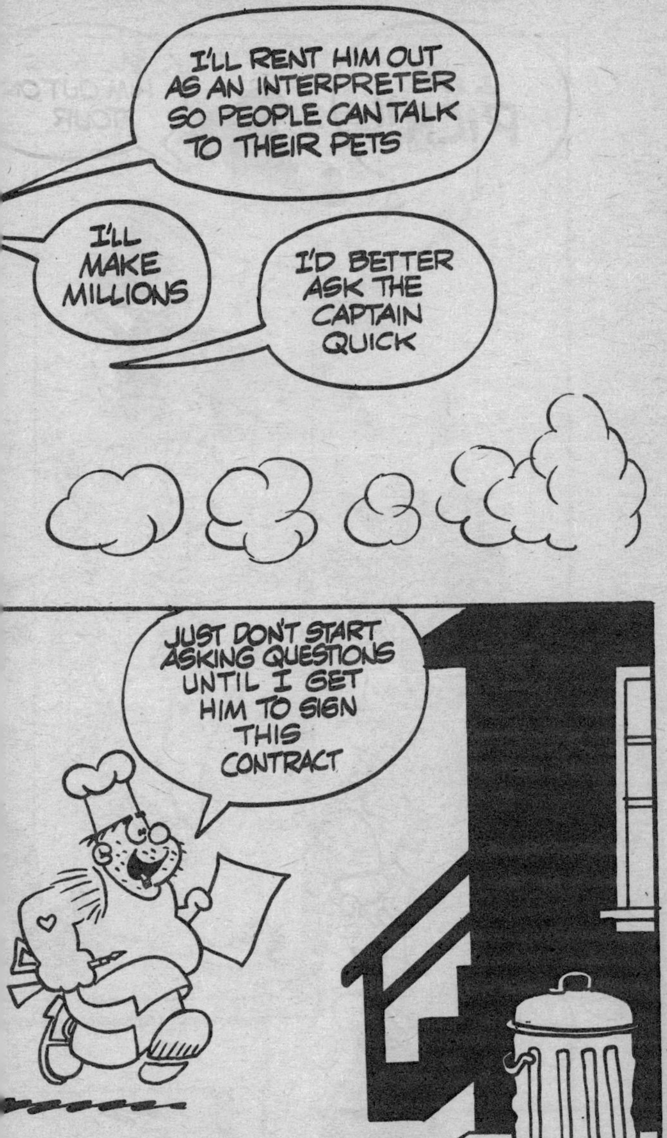
I'LL RENT HIM OUT AS AN INTERPRETER SO PEOPLE CAN TALK TO THEIR PETS
I'LL MAKE MILLIONS
I'D BETTER ASK THE CAPTAIN QUICK
JUST DON'T START ASKING QUESTIONS UNTIL I GET HIM TO SIGN THIS CONTRACT

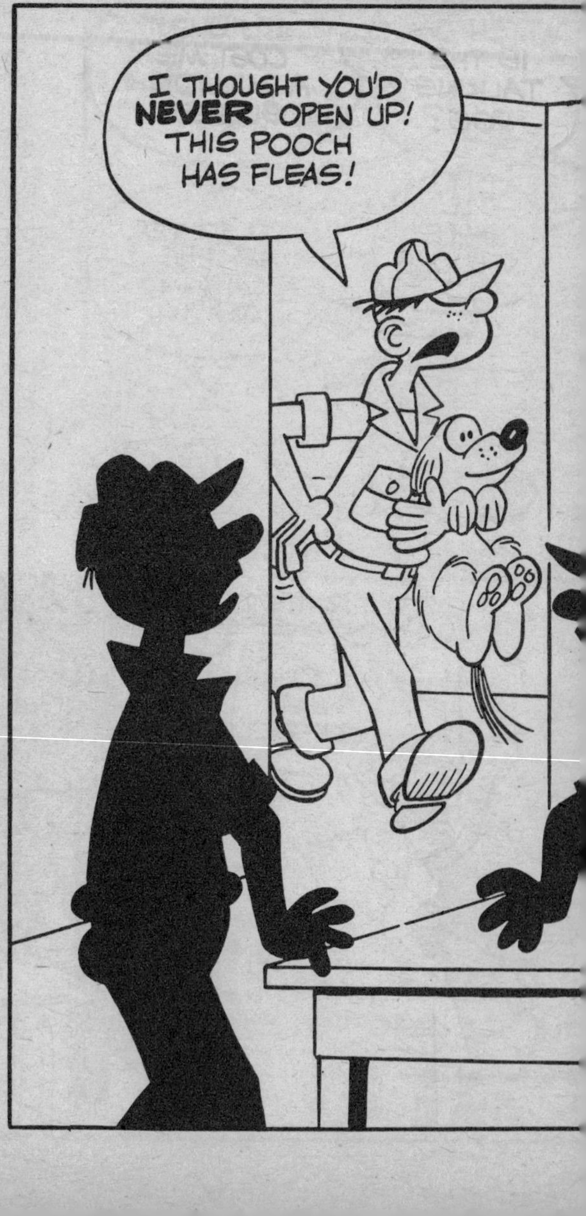
I THOUGHT YOU'D **NEVER** OPEN UP! THIS POOCH HAS FLEAS!

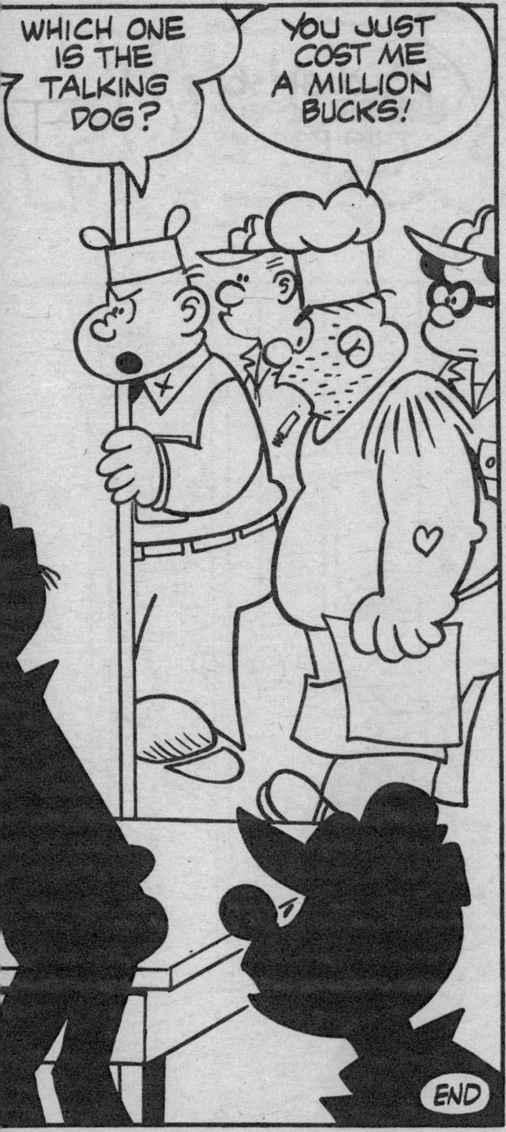
WHICH ONE IS THE TALKING DOG?
YOU JUST COST ME A MILLION BUCKS!
END

The SQUEAKY

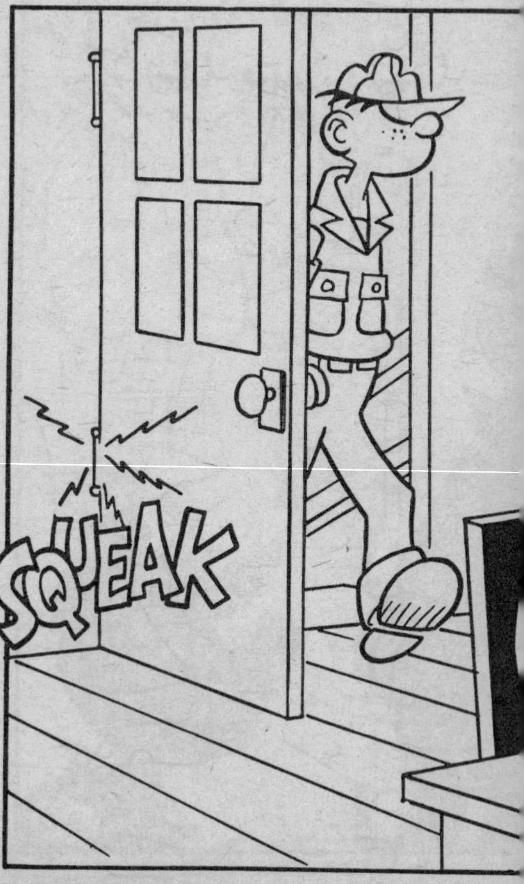
SQUEAK

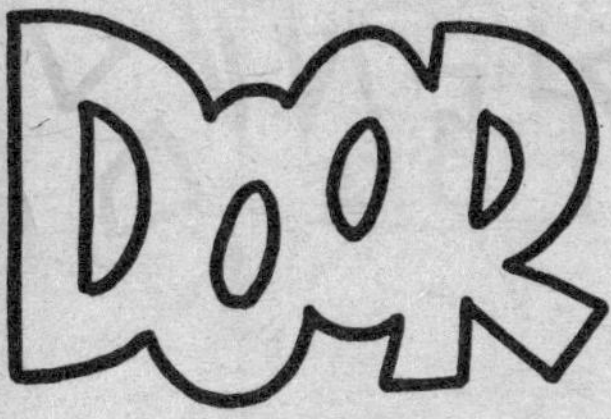
DOOR

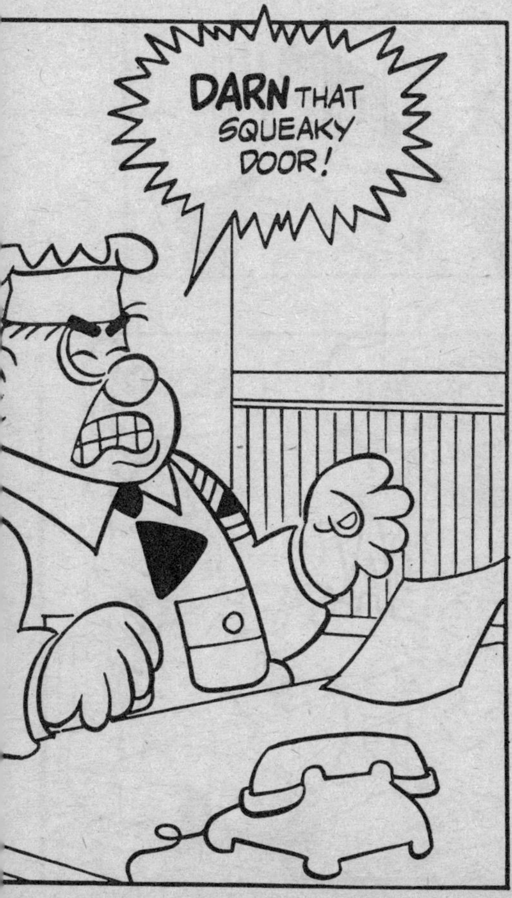
DARN THAT SQUEAKY DOOR!

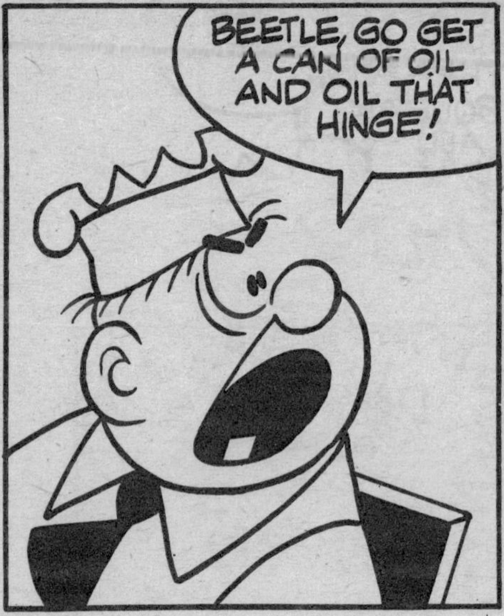
BEETLE, GO GET A CAN OF OIL AND OIL THAT HINGE!

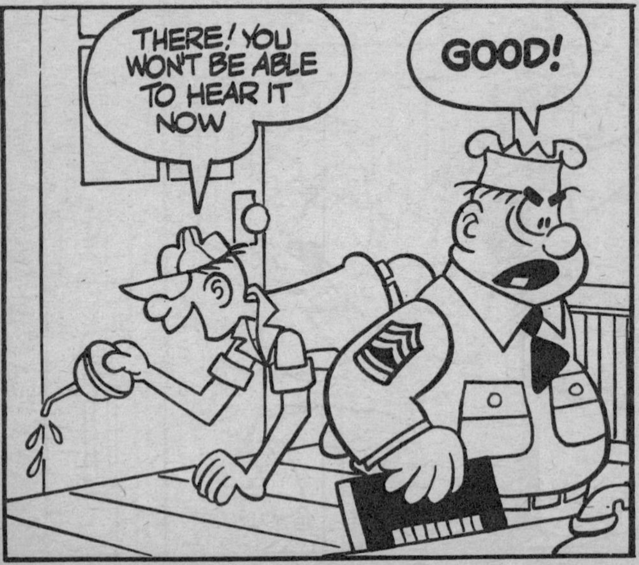
THERE! YOU WON'T BE ABLE TO HEAR IT NOW
GOOD!

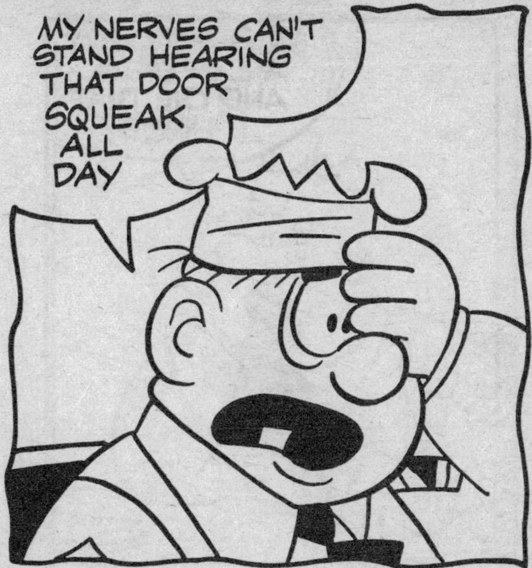
MY NERVES CAN'T STAND HEARING THAT DOOR SQUEAK ALL DAY

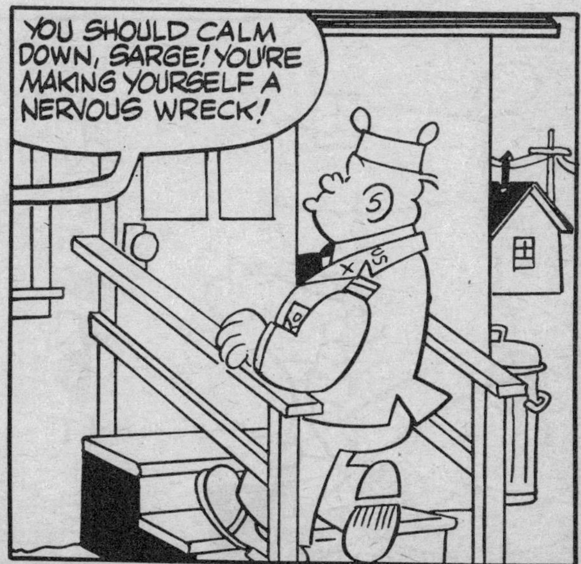
YOU SHOULD CALM DOWN, SARGE! YOU'RE MAKING YOURSELF A NERVOUS WRECK!

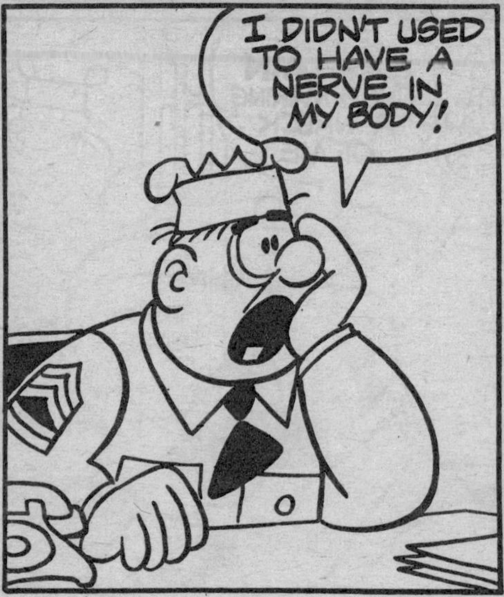
I DIDN'T USED TO HAVE A NERVE IN MY BODY!

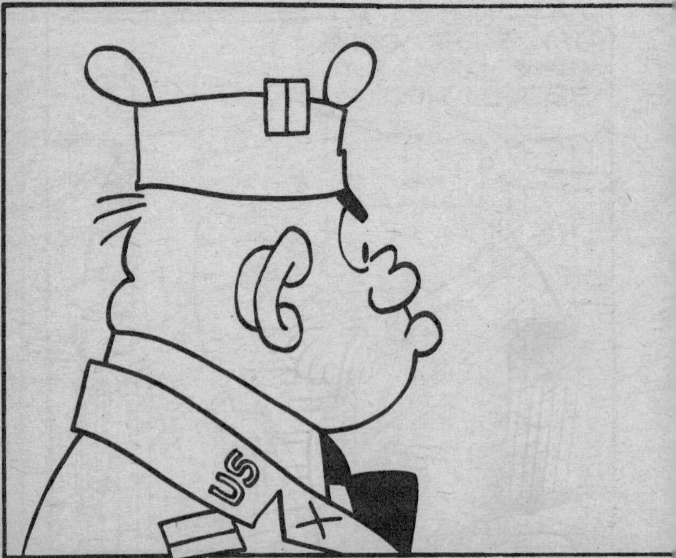
US

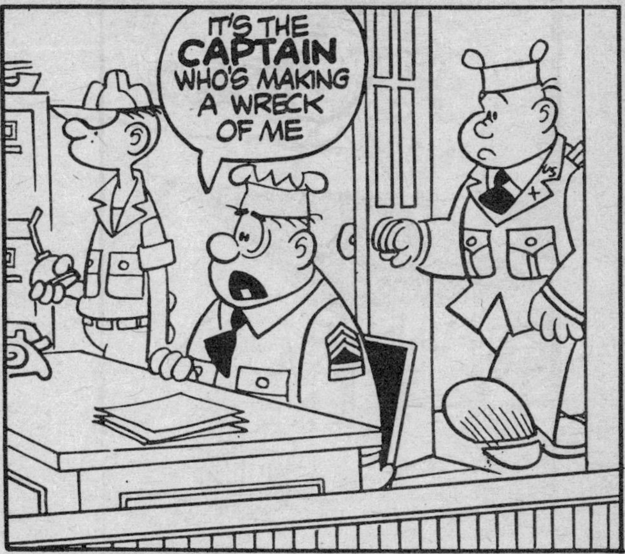
IT'S THE CAPTAIN WHO'S MAKING A WRECK OF ME

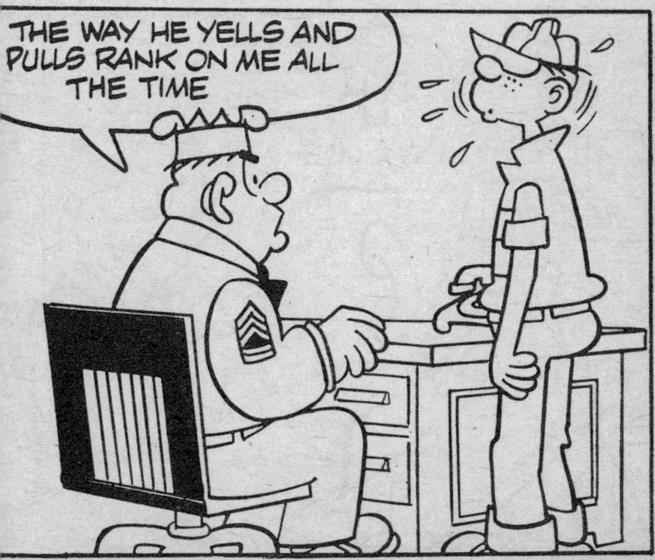
THE WAY HE YELLS AND PULLS RANK ON ME ALL THE TIME

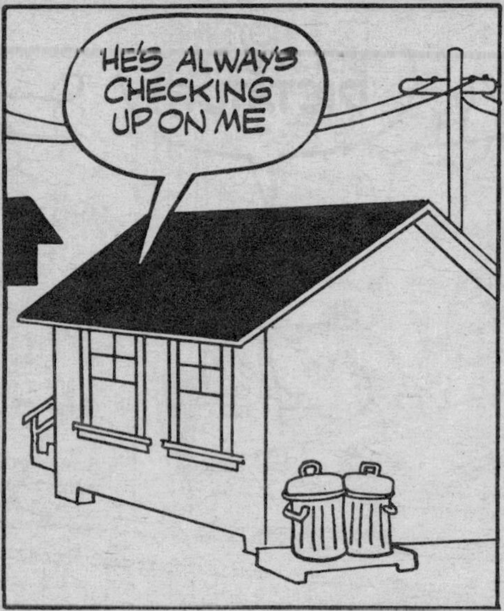
HE'S ALWAYS CHECKING UP ON ME

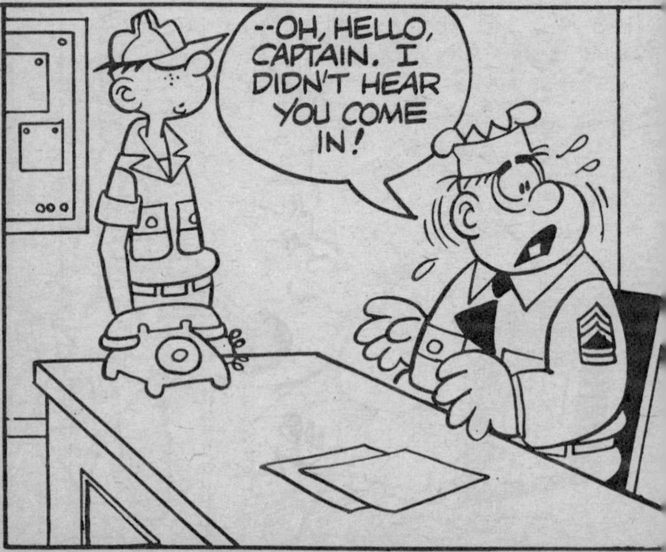
--OH, HELLO, CAPTAIN. I DIDN'T HEAR YOU COME IN!

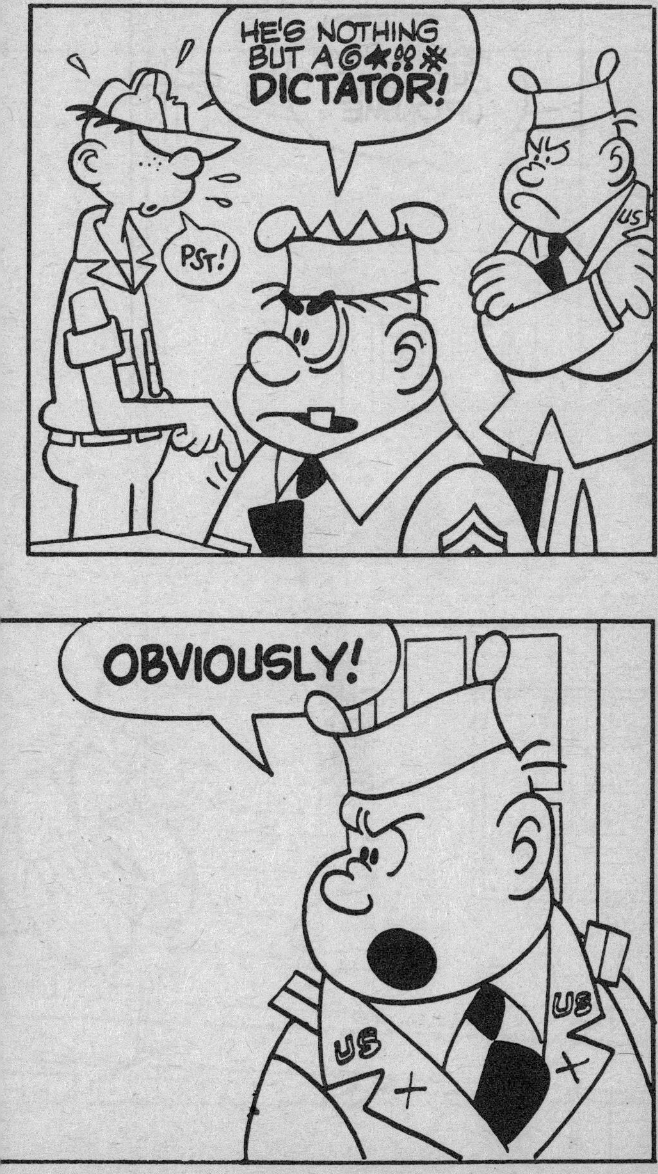
HE'S NOTHING BUT A @★!!✱ DICTATOR!
PST!
OBVIOUSLY!

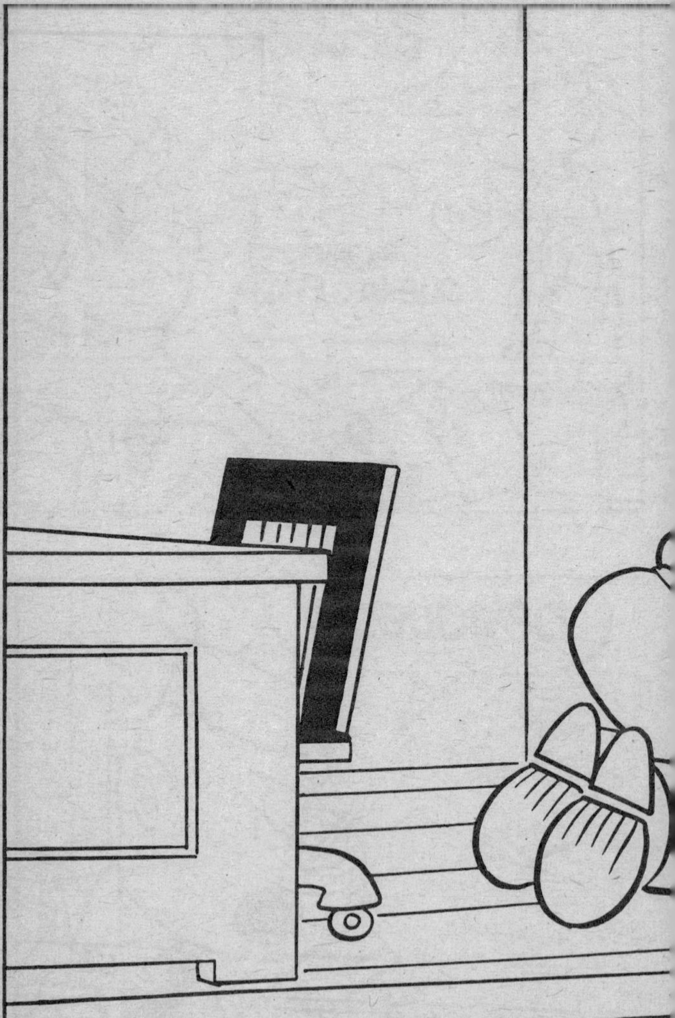

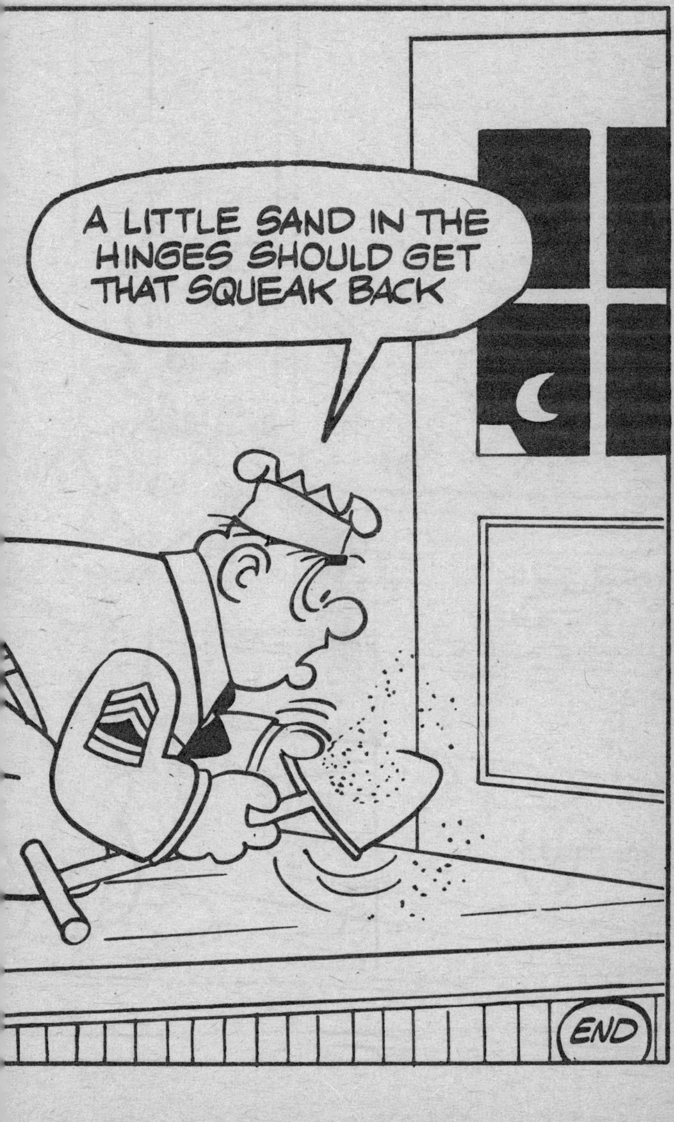
A LITTLE SAND IN THE HINGES SHOULD GET THAT SQUEAK BACK
END

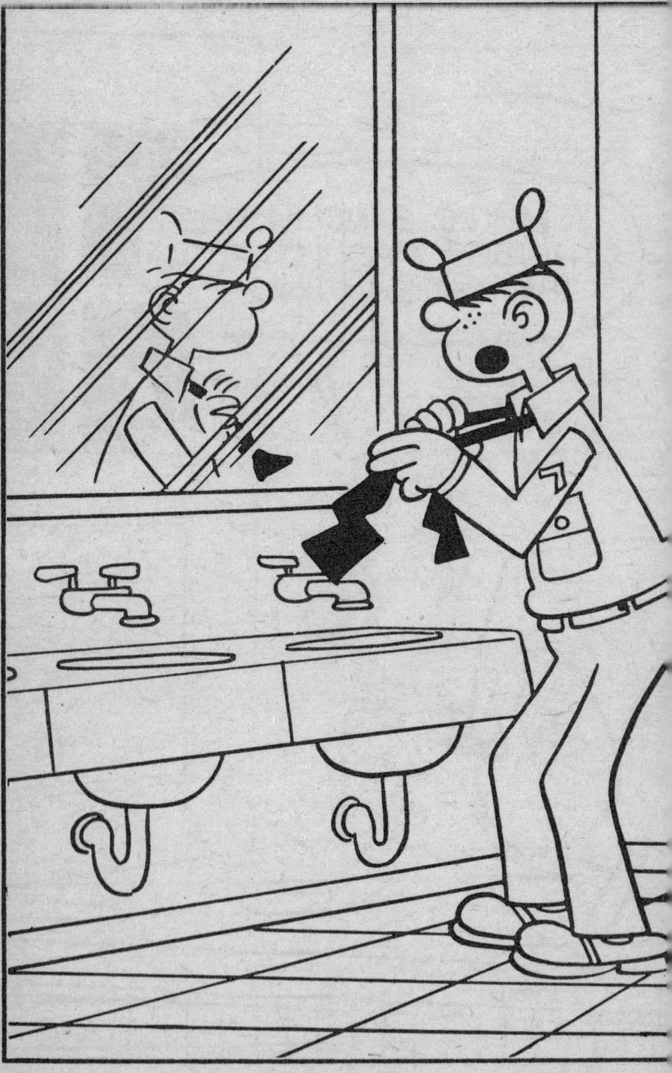

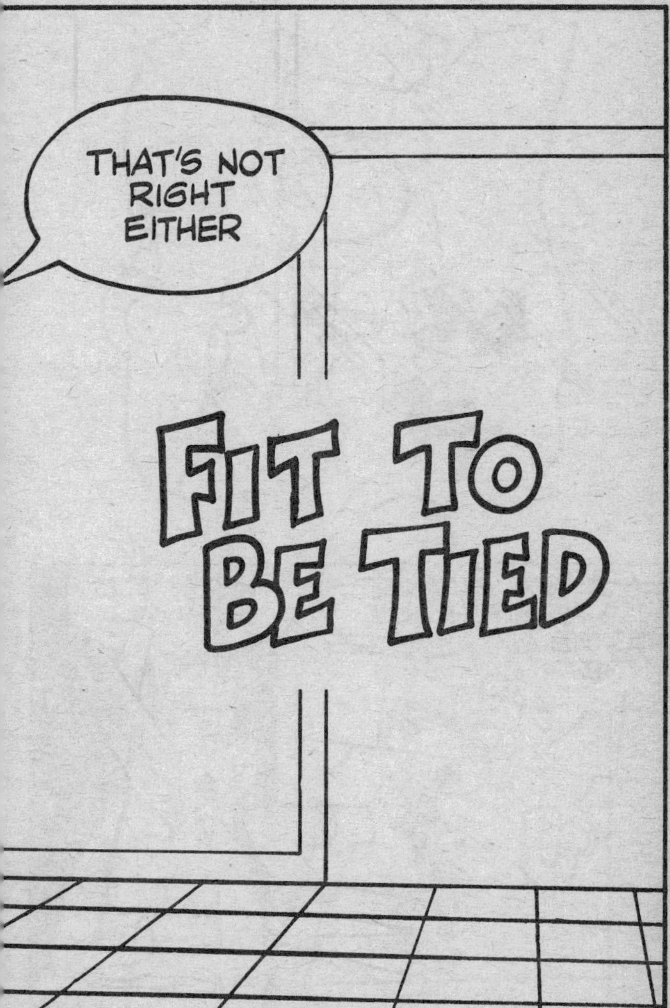
THAT'S NOT RIGHT EITHER
FIT TO BE TIED

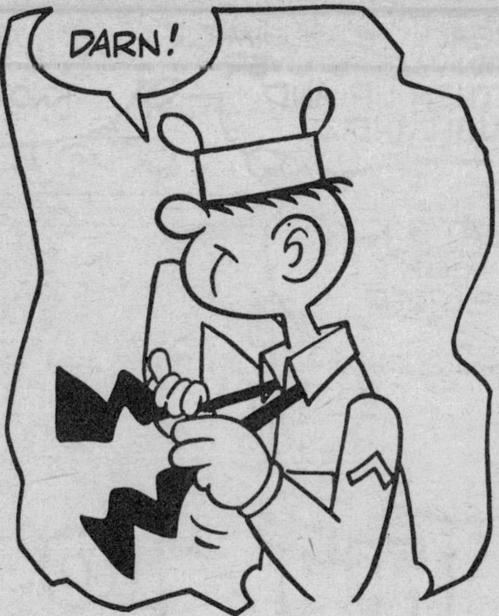
DARN!

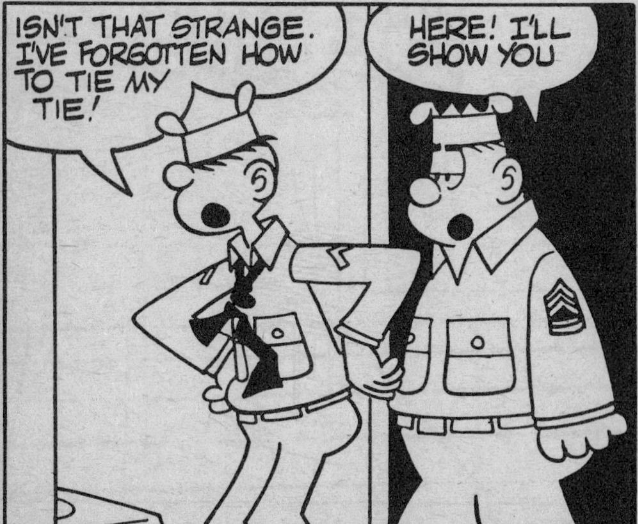
ISN'T THAT STRANGE. I'VE FORGOTTEN HOW TO TIE MY TIE!
HERE! I'LL SHOW YOU

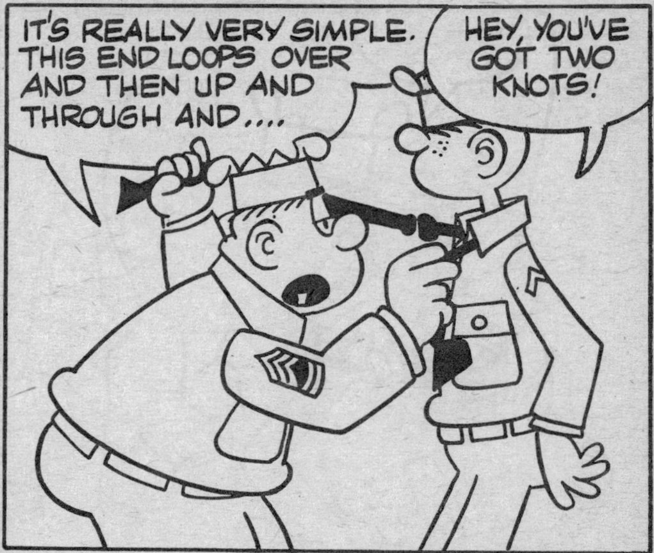
IT'S REALLY VERY SIMPLE. THIS END LOOPS OVER AND THEN UP AND THROUGH AND....
HEY, YOU'VE GOT TWO KNOTS!

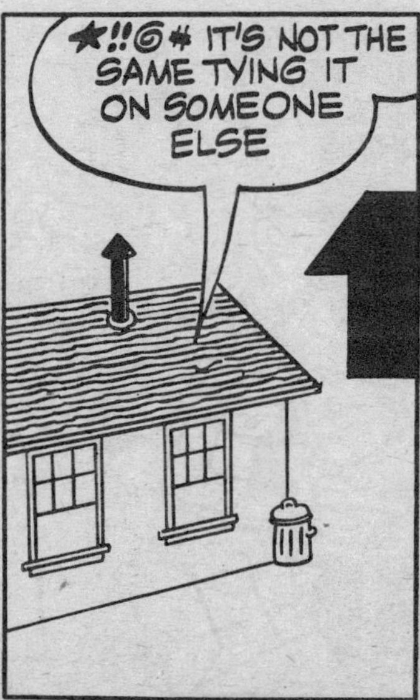
*!!@# IT'S NOT THE SAME TYING IT ON SOMEONE ELSE

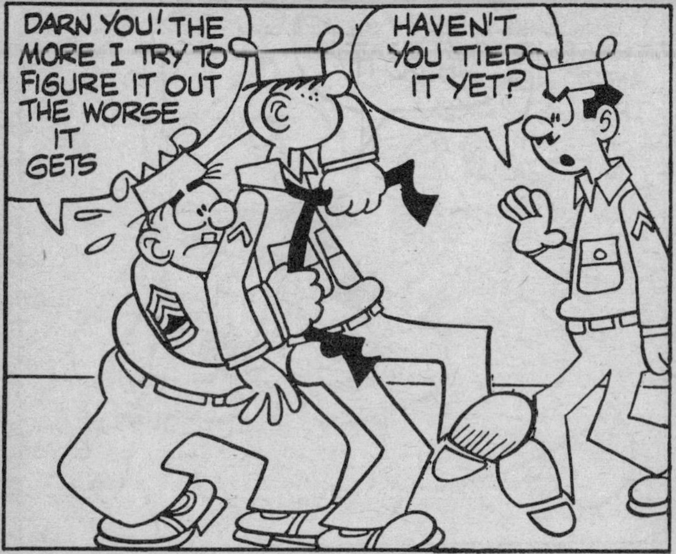
DARN YOU! THE MORE I TRY TO FIGURE IT OUT THE WORSE IT GETS
HAVEN'T YOU TIED IT YET?

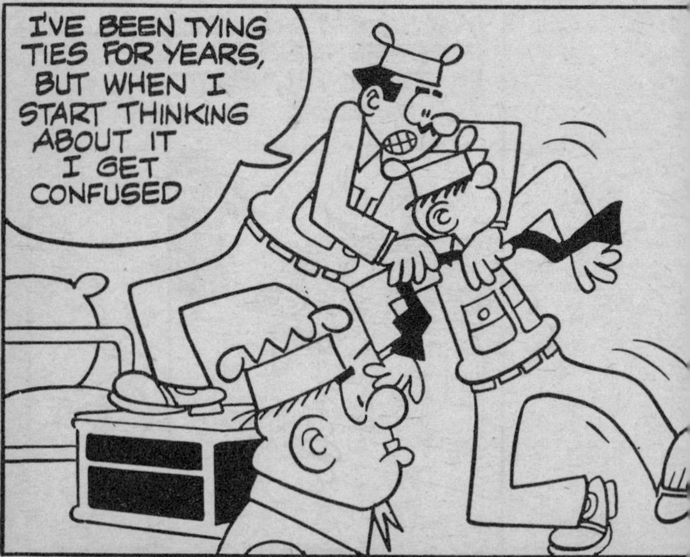
I'VE BEEN TYING TIES FOR YEARS, BUT WHEN I START THINKING ABOUT IT I GET CONFUSED

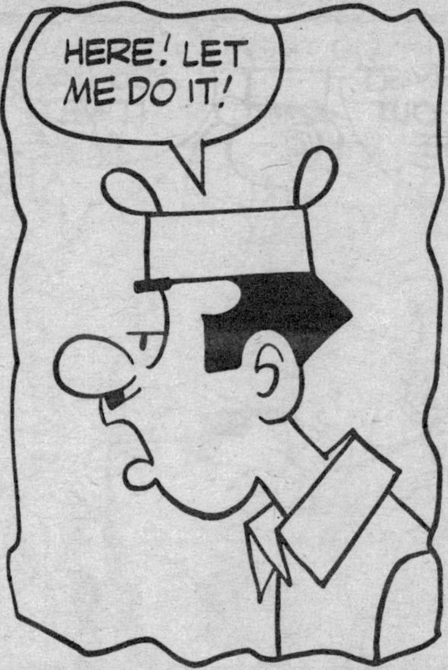
HERE! LET ME DO IT!

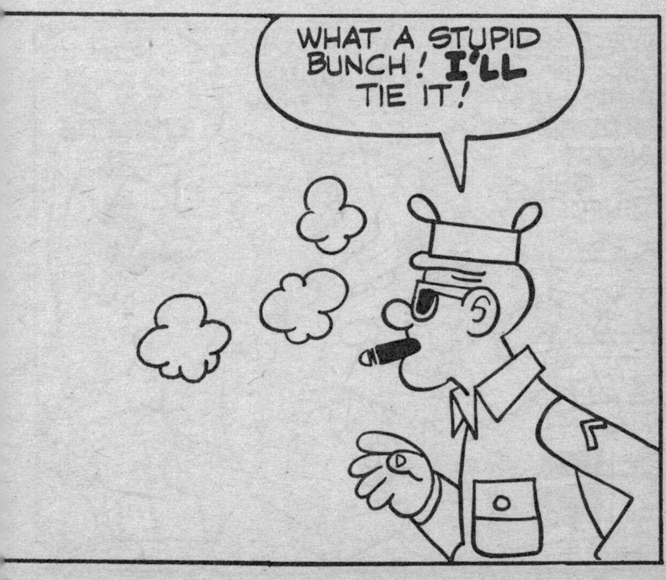
WHAT A STUPID BUNCH! **I'LL** TIE IT!

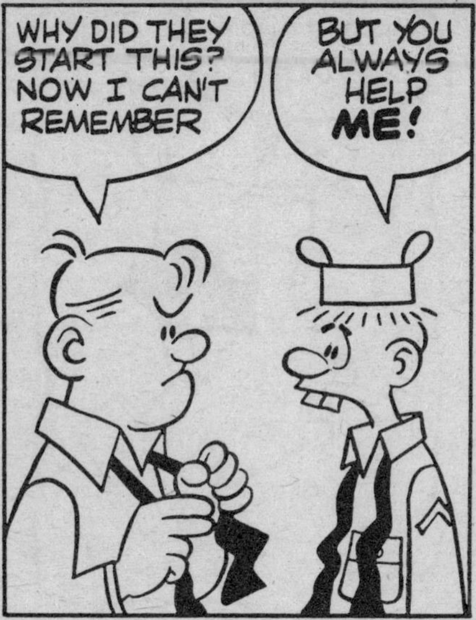
WHY DID THEY START THIS? NOW I CAN'T REMEMBER
BUT YOU ALWAYS HELP **ME**!

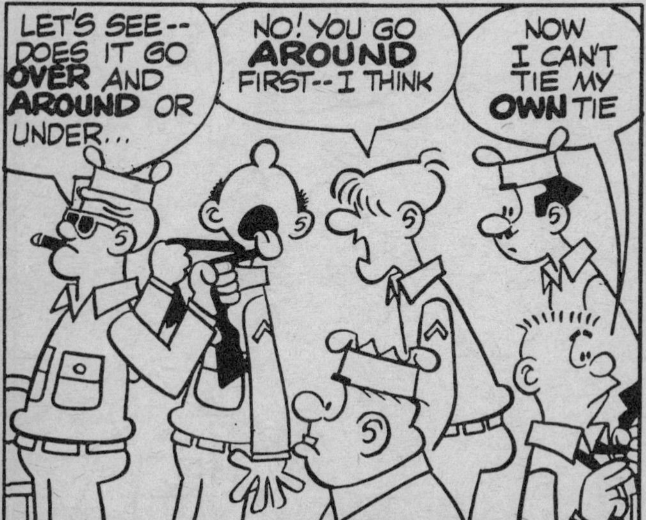
LET'S SEE-- DOES IT GO **OVER** AND **AROUND** OR UNDER...
NO! YOU GO **AROUND** FIRST--I THINK
NOW I CAN'T TIE MY **OWN** TIE

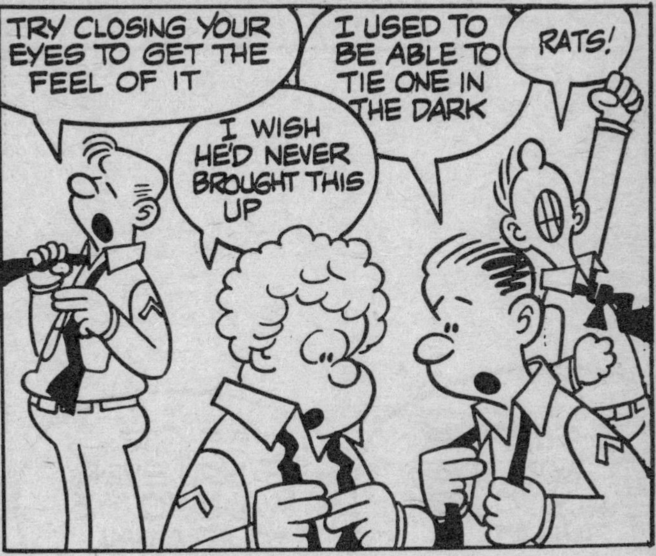
TRY CLOSING YOUR EYES TO GET THE FEEL OF IT
I WISH HE'D NEVER BROUGHT THIS UP
I USED TO BE ABLE TO TIE ONE IN THE DARK
RATS!

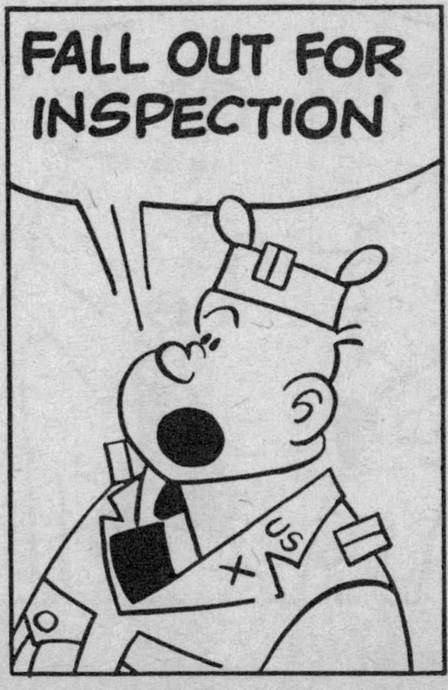
FALL OUT FOR INSPECTION

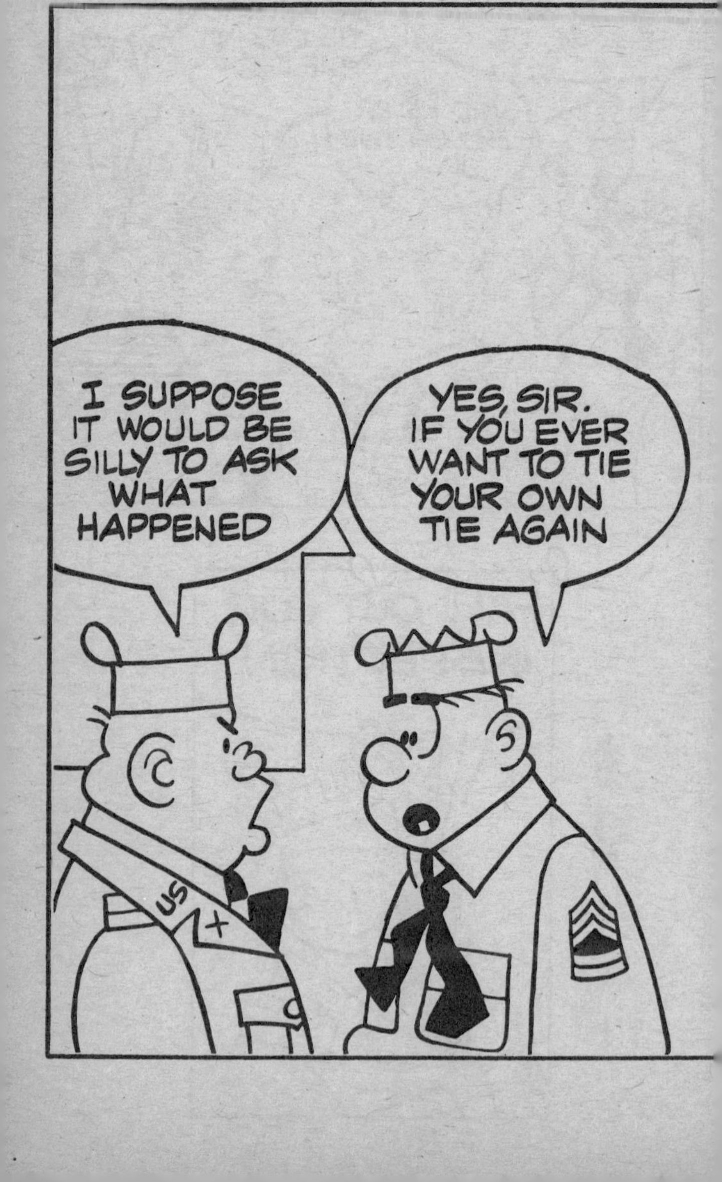
I SUPPOSE IT WOULD BE SILLY TO ASK WHAT HAPPENED
YES, SIR. IF YOU EVER WANT TO TIE YOUR OWN TIE AGAIN
US

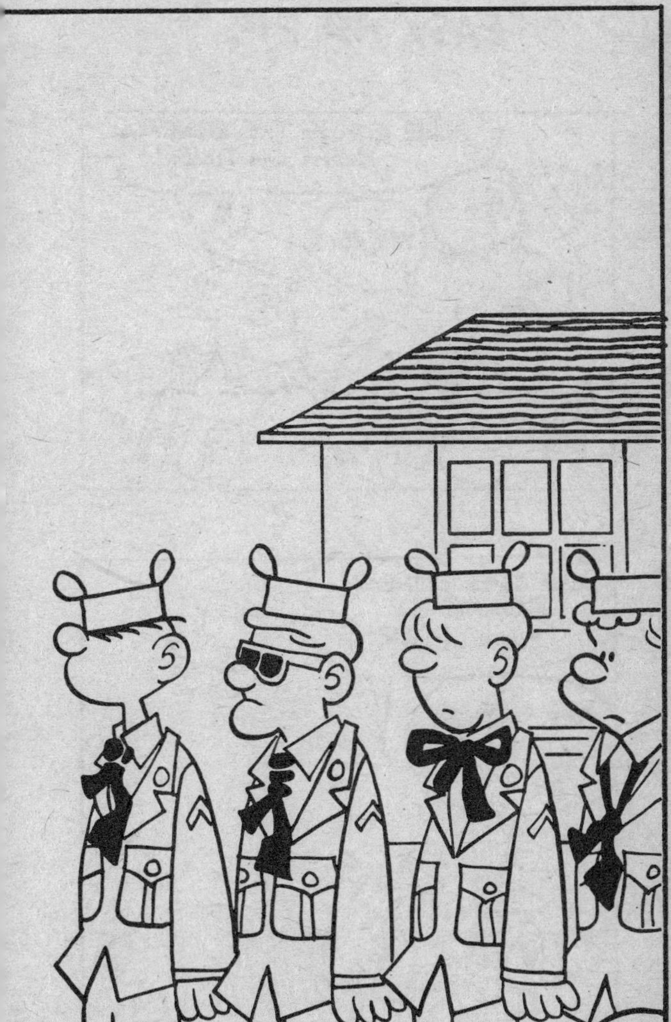
END

"EASY AS PIE"

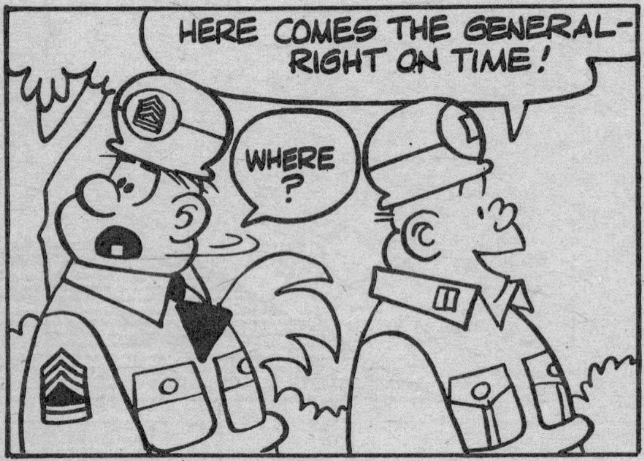
HERE COMES THE GENERAL-
RIGHT ON TIME!
WHERE
?

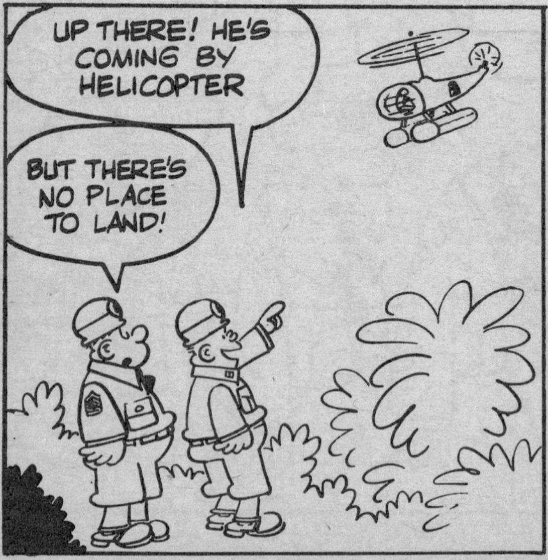
UP THERE! HE'S
COMING BY
HELICOPTER
BUT THERE'S
NO PLACE
TO LAND!

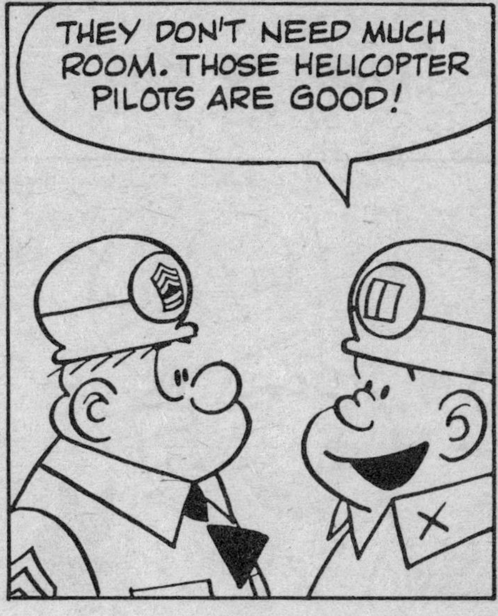
THEY DON'T NEED MUCH ROOM. THOSE HELICOPTER PILOTS ARE GOOD!

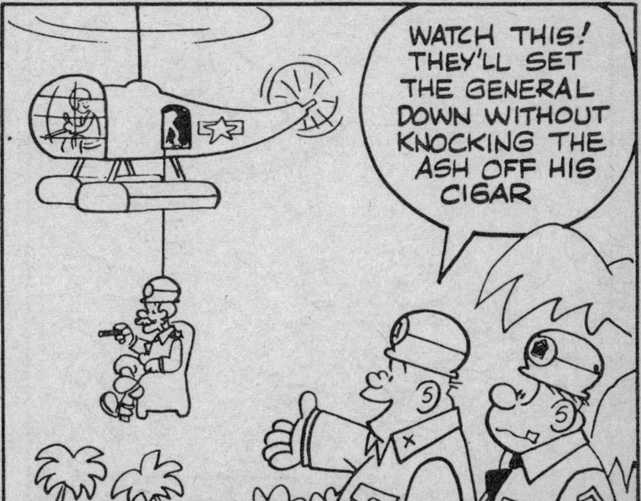
WATCH THIS! THEY'LL SET THE GENERAL DOWN WITHOUT KNOCKING THE ASH OFF HIS CIGAR

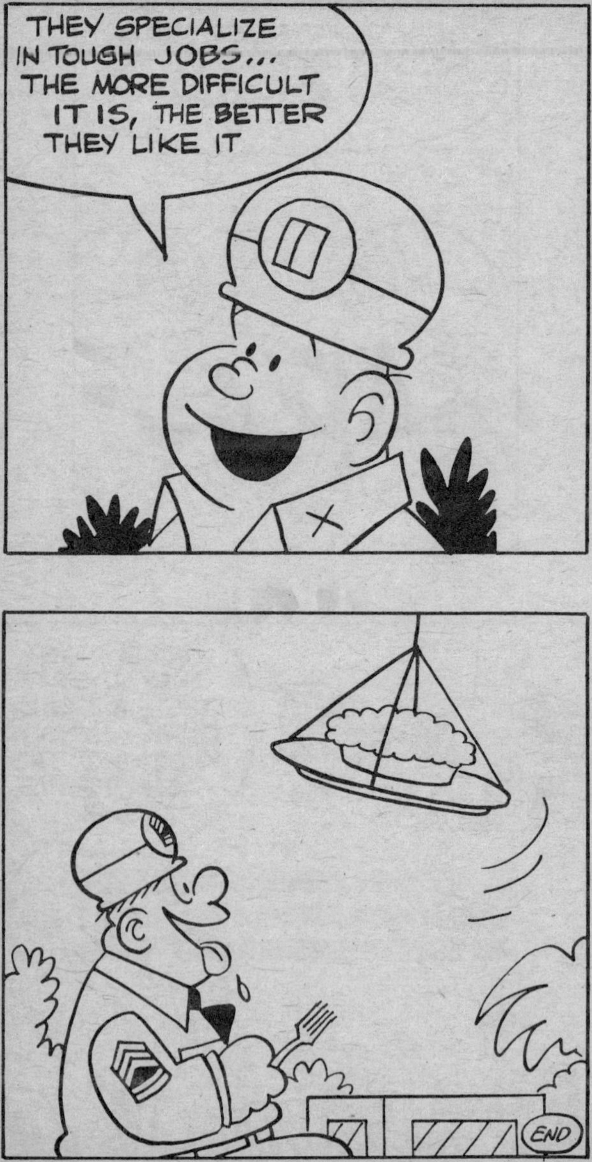
THEY SPECIALIZE IN TOUGH JOBS... THE MORE DIFFICULT IT IS, THE BETTER THEY LIKE IT
END

SARGE
and
STRIPES

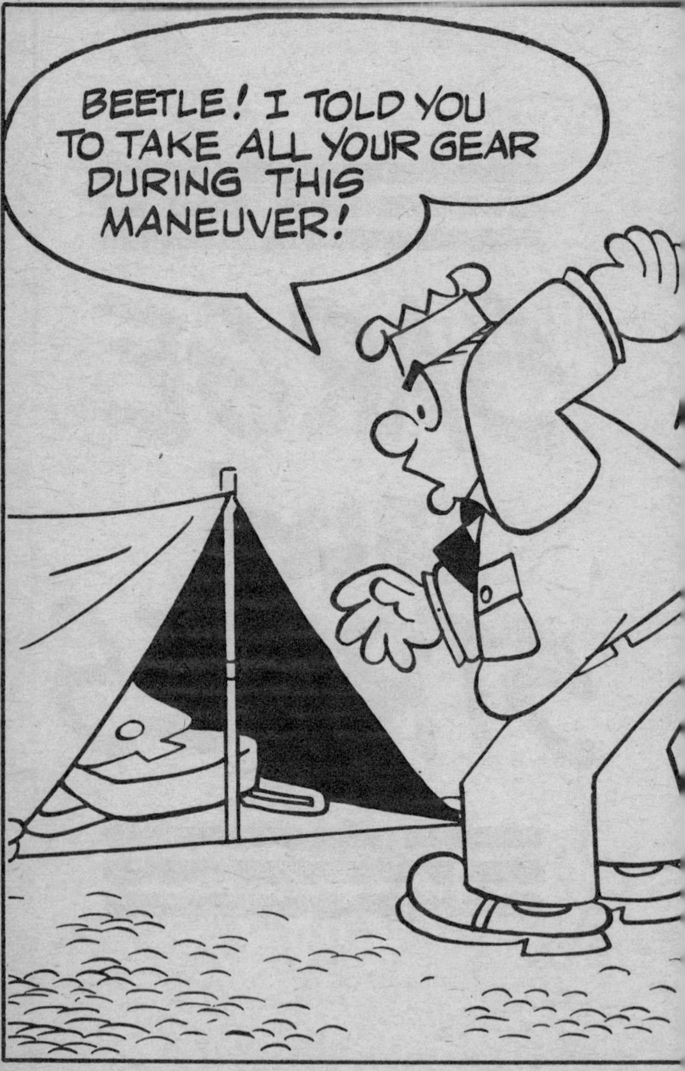
BEETLE! I TOLD YOU TO TAKE ALL YOUR GEAR DURING THIS MANEUVER!

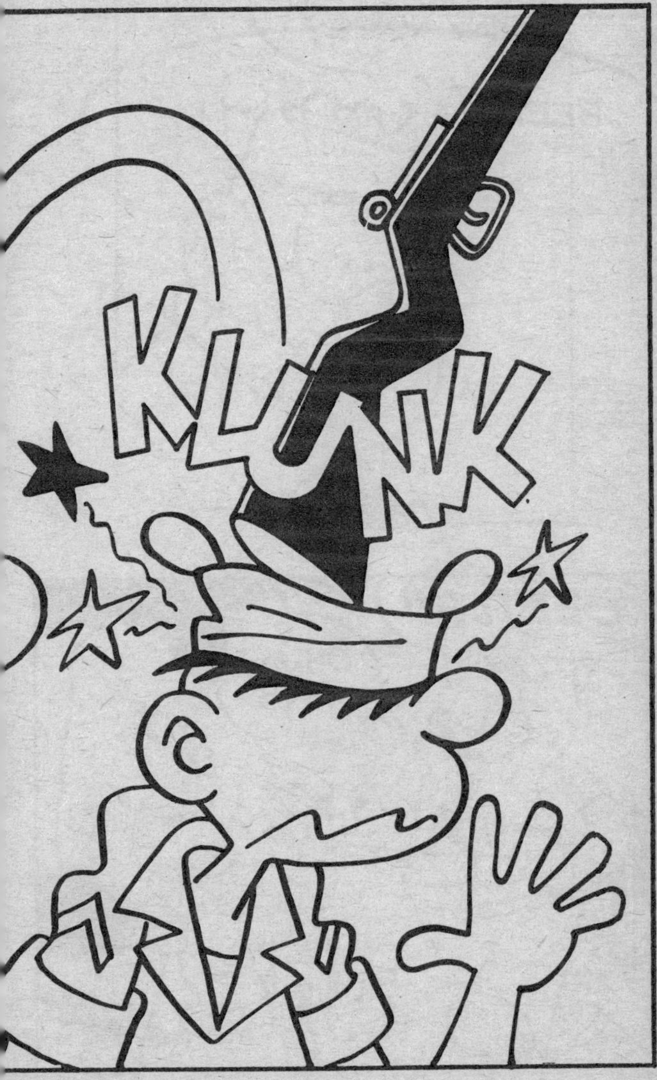
KLUNK

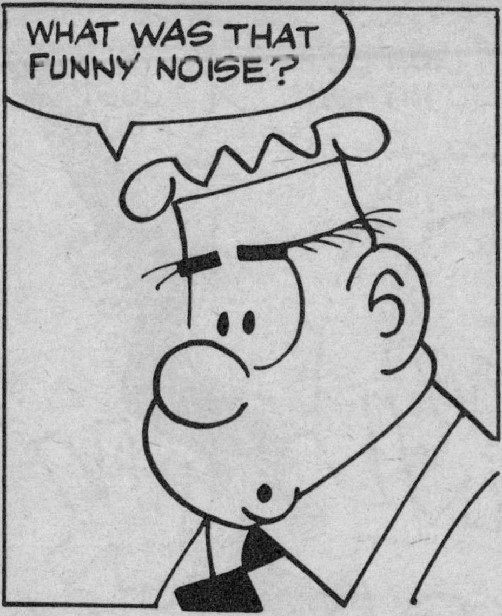
WHAT WAS THAT FUNNY NOISE?

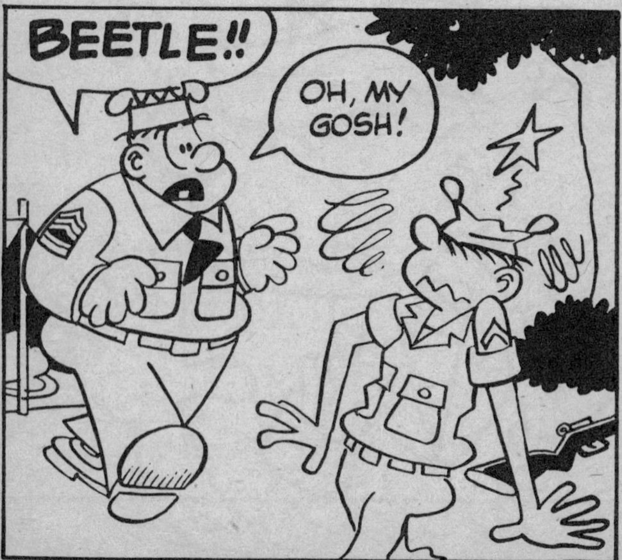
BEETLE!!
OH, MY GOSH!

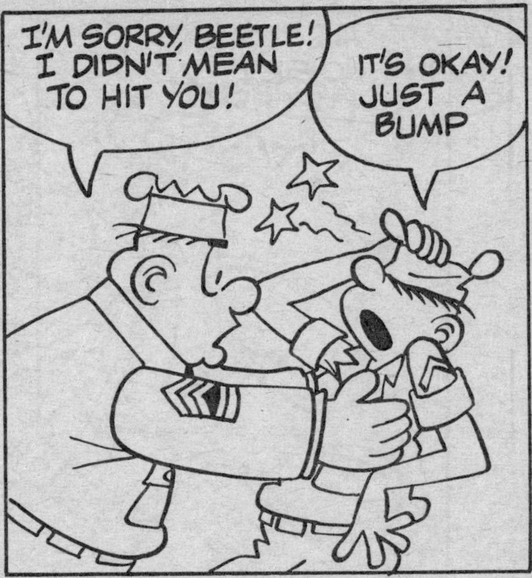
I'M SORRY, BEETLE! I DIDN'T MEAN TO HIT YOU!
IT'S OKAY! JUST A BUMP

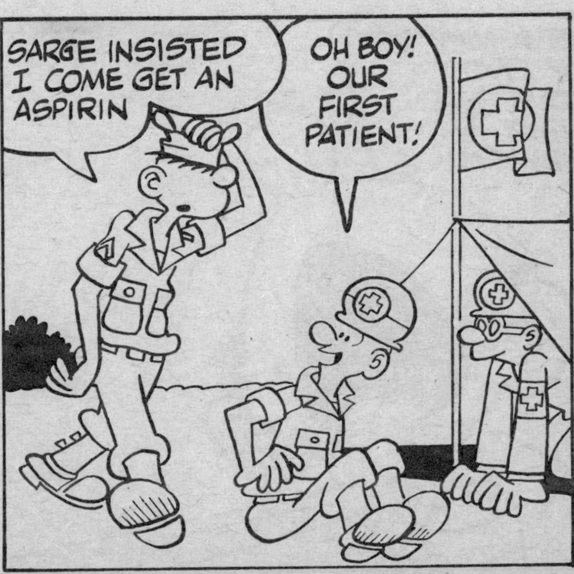
SARGE INSISTED I COME GET AN ASPIRIN
OH BOY! OUR FIRST PATIENT!

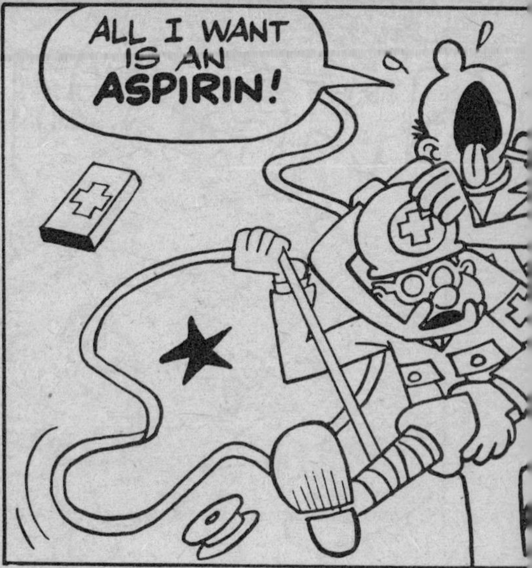
ALL I WANT IS AN ASPIRIN!

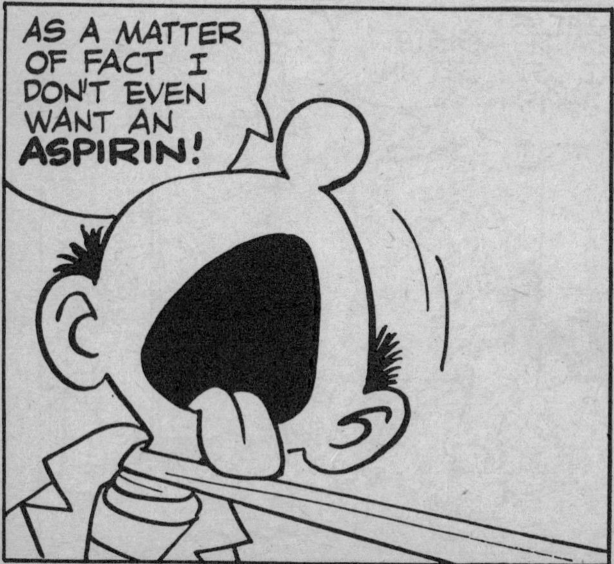
AS A MATTER OF FACT I DON'T EVEN WANT AN ASPIRIN!

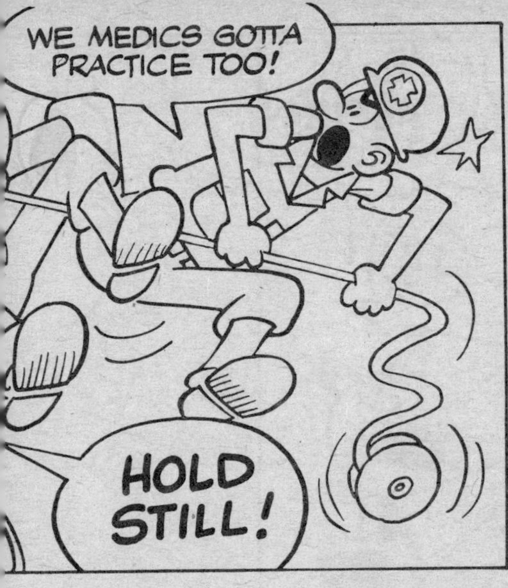
WE MEDICS GOTTA PRACTICE TOO!
HOLD STILL!

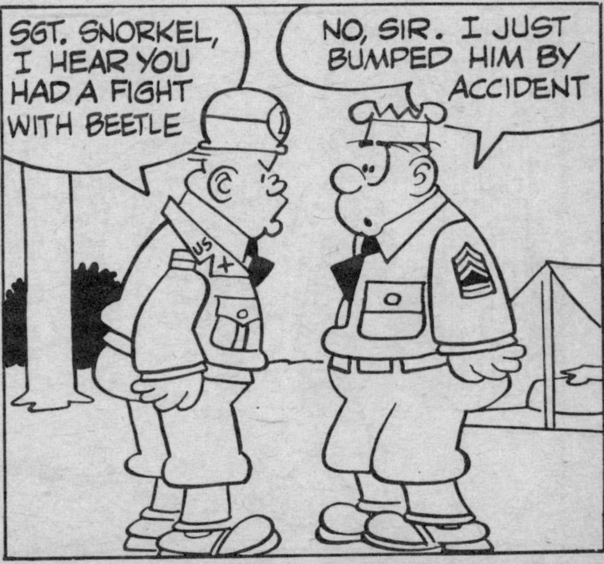
SGT. SNORKEL, I HEAR YOU HAD A FIGHT WITH BEETLE
NO, SIR. I JUST BUMPED HIM BY ACCIDENT
US

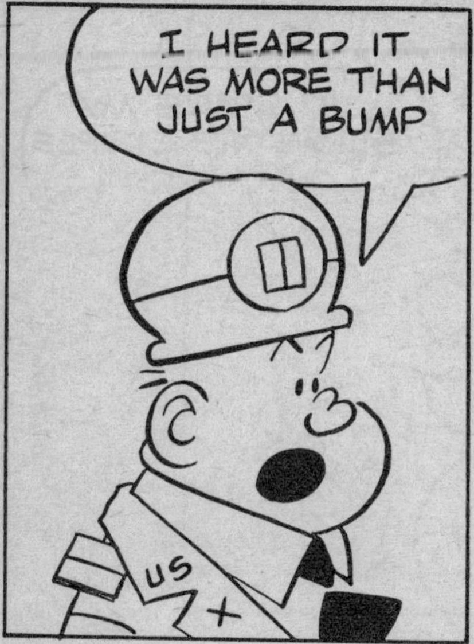
I HEARD IT WAS MORE THAN JUST A BUMP

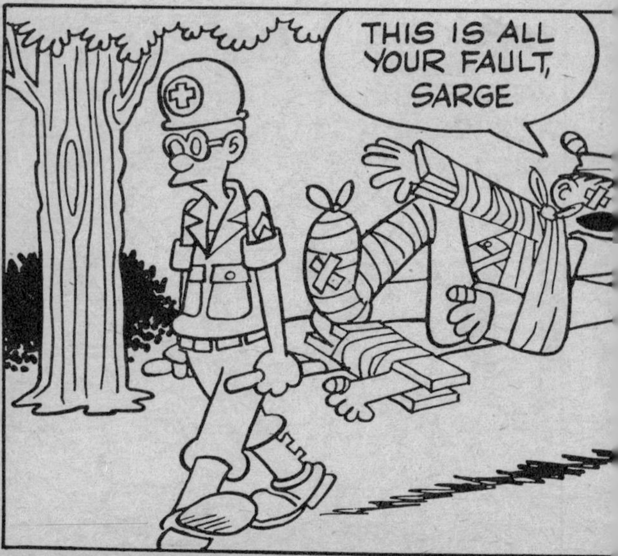
THIS IS ALL YOUR FAULT, SARGE

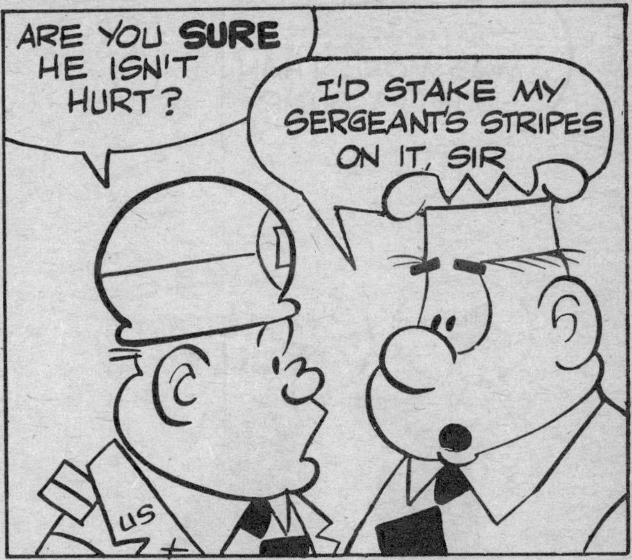
ARE YOU **SURE** HE ISN'T HURT?
I'D STAKE MY SERGEANT'S STRIPES ON IT, SIR

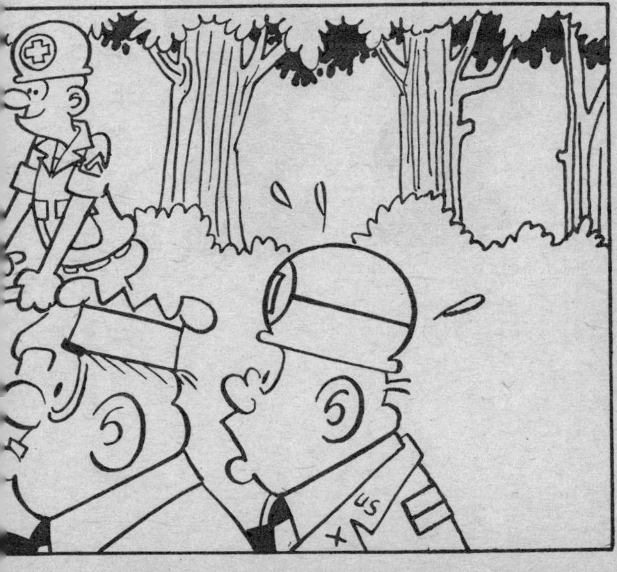

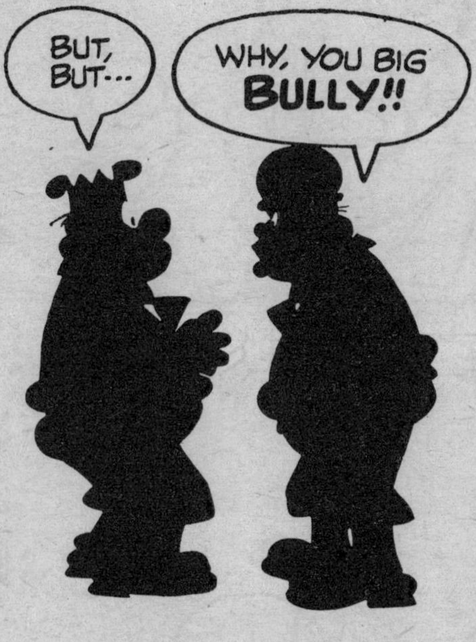
BUT, BUT...
WHY, YOU BIG BULLY!!

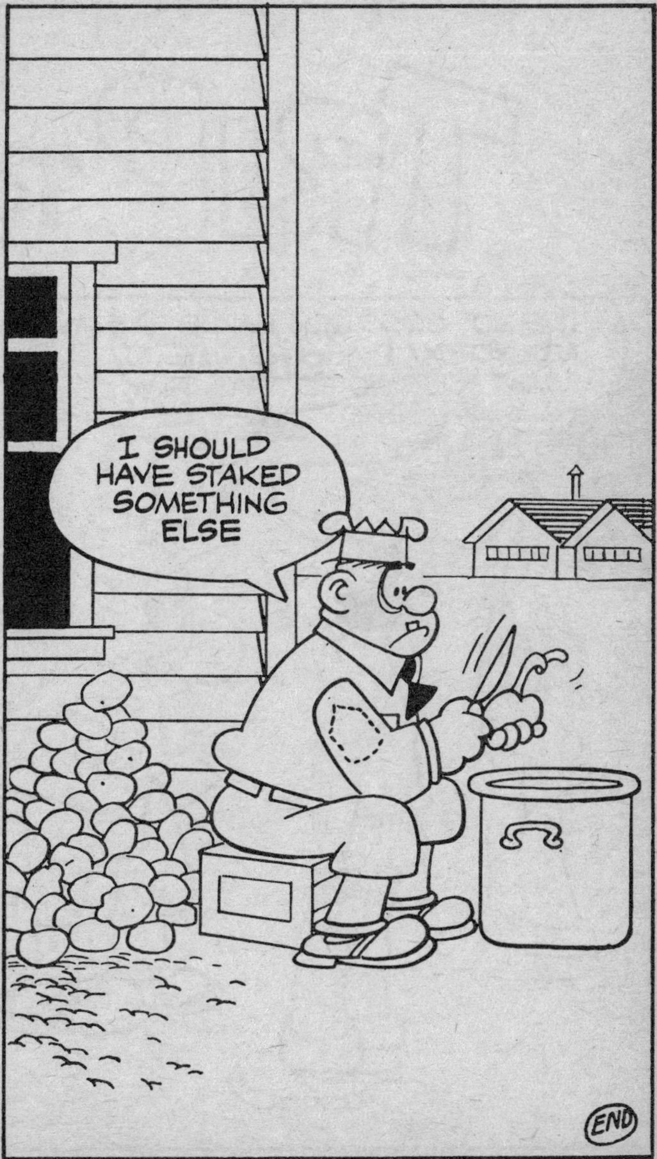
I SHOULD HAVE STAKED SOMETHING ELSE
END

TRIP To

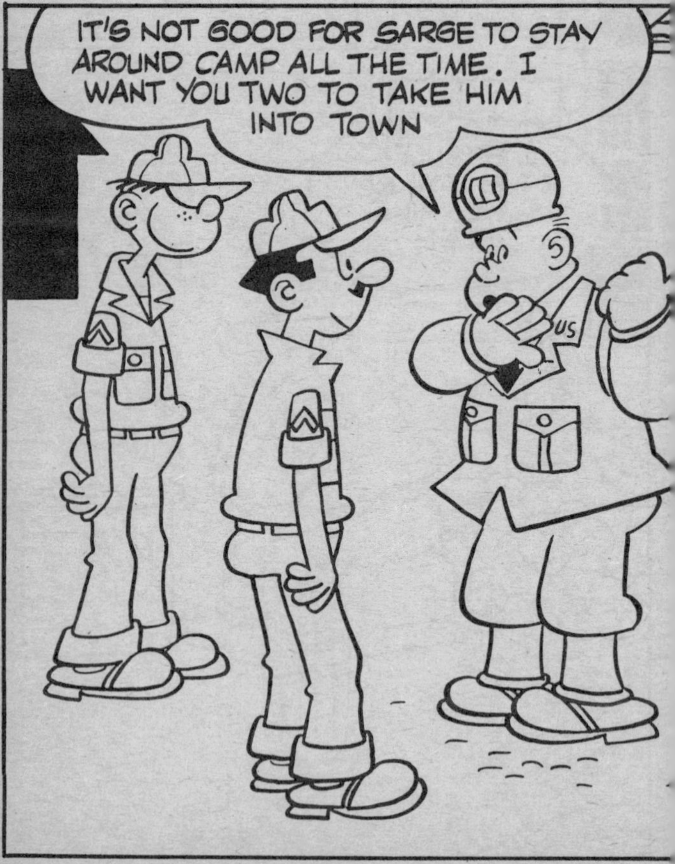
IT'S NOT GOOD FOR SARGE TO STAY AROUND CAMP ALL THE TIME. I WANT YOU TWO TO TAKE HIM INTO TOWN

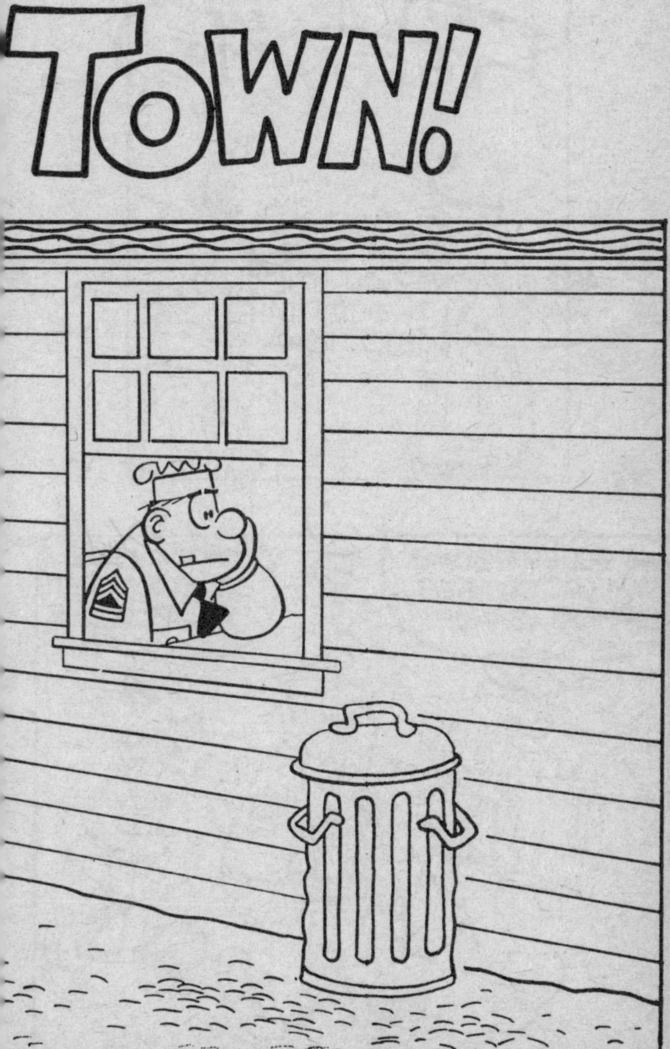
TOWN!

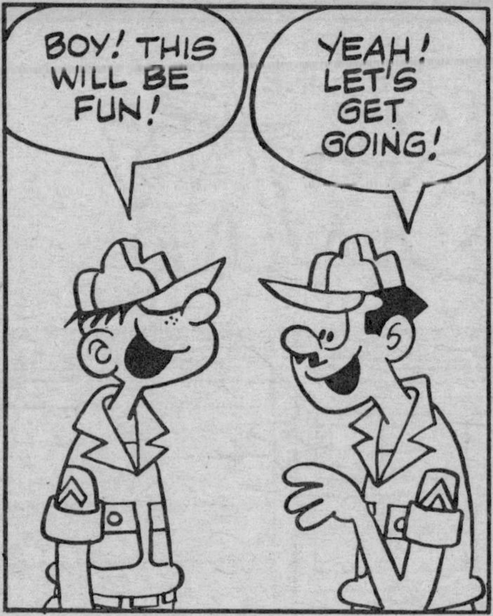
BOY! THIS WILL BE FUN!
YEAH! LET'S GET GOING!

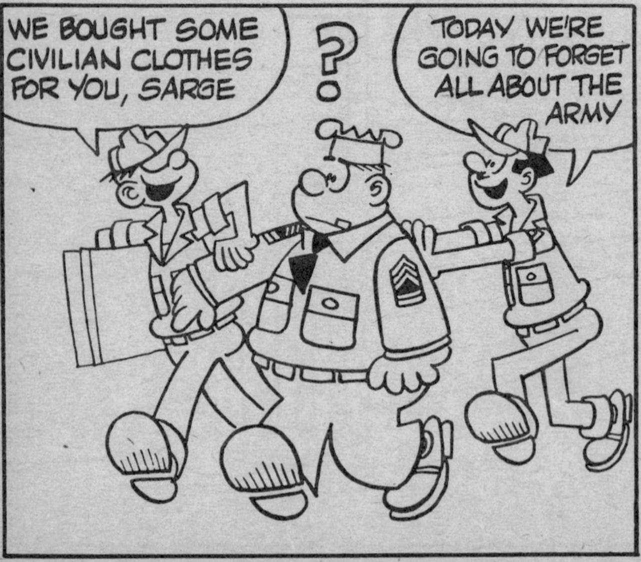
WE BOUGHT SOME CIVILIAN CLOTHES FOR YOU, SARGE
?
TODAY WE'RE GOING TO FORGET ALL ABOUT THE ARMY

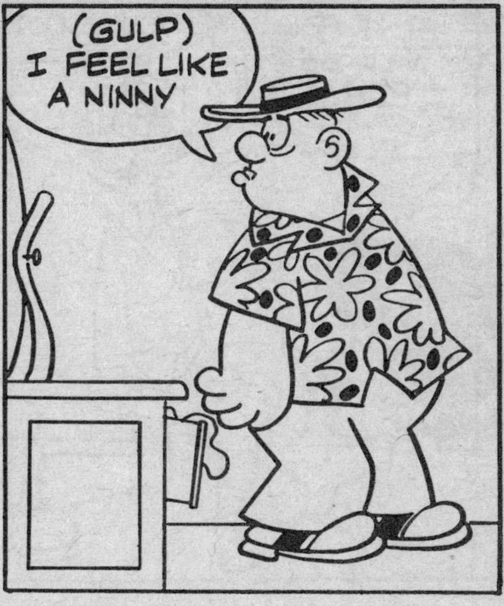
(GULP) I FEEL LIKE A NINNY

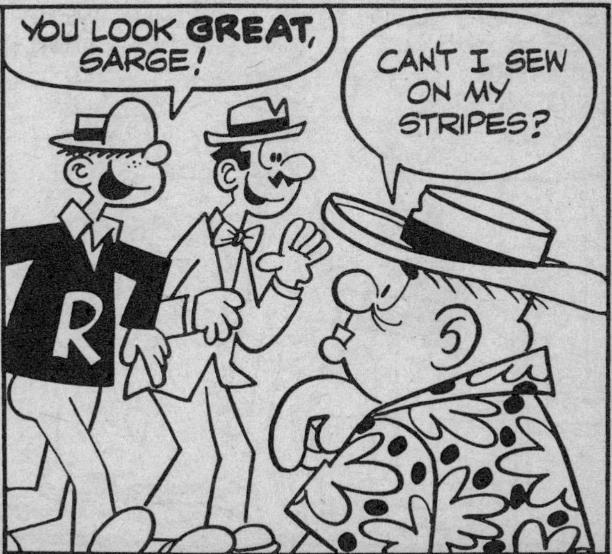
YOU LOOK **GREAT**, SARGE!
CAN'T I SEW ON MY STRIPES?

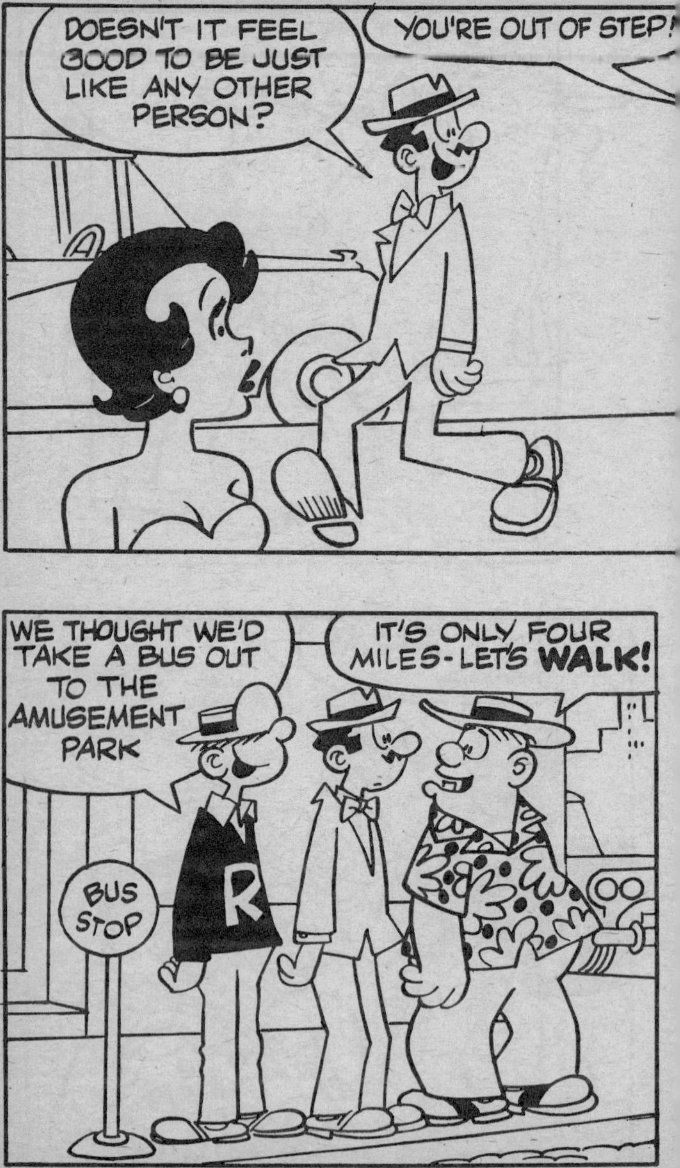
DOESN'T IT FEEL GOOD TO BE JUST LIKE ANY OTHER PERSON?
YOU'RE OUT OF STEP!
WE THOUGHT WE'D TAKE A BUS OUT TO THE AMUSEMENT PARK
IT'S ONLY FOUR MILES-LET'S **WALK!**
BUS STOP

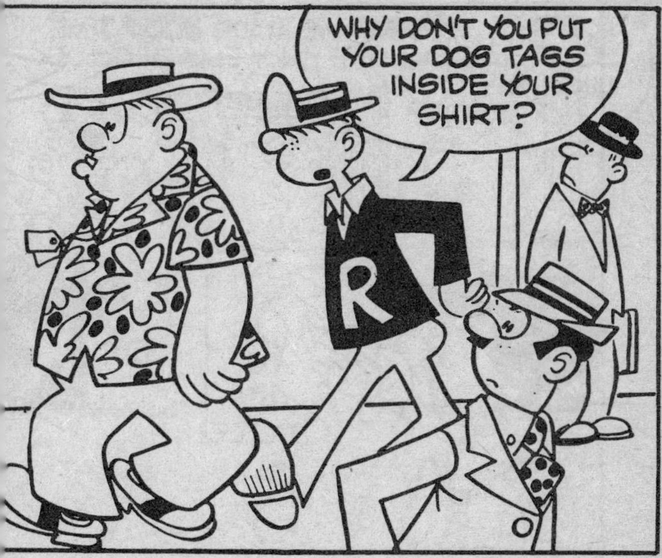
WHY DON'T YOU PUT YOUR DOG TAGS INSIDE YOUR SHIRT?

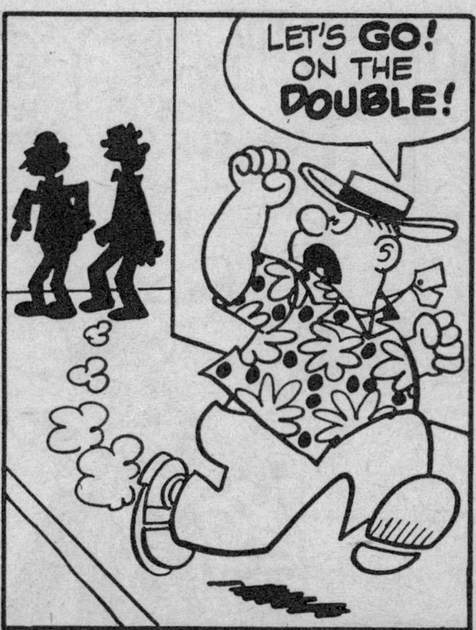
LET'S GO! ON THE DOUBLE!

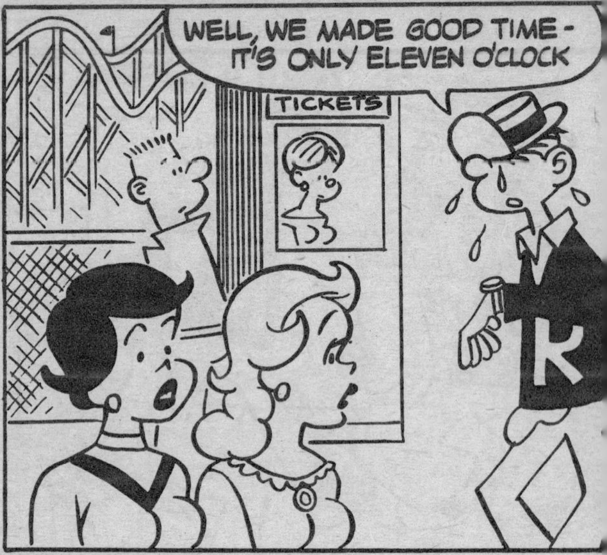
WELL, WE MADE GOOD TIME - IT'S ONLY ELEVEN O'CLOCK
TICKETS

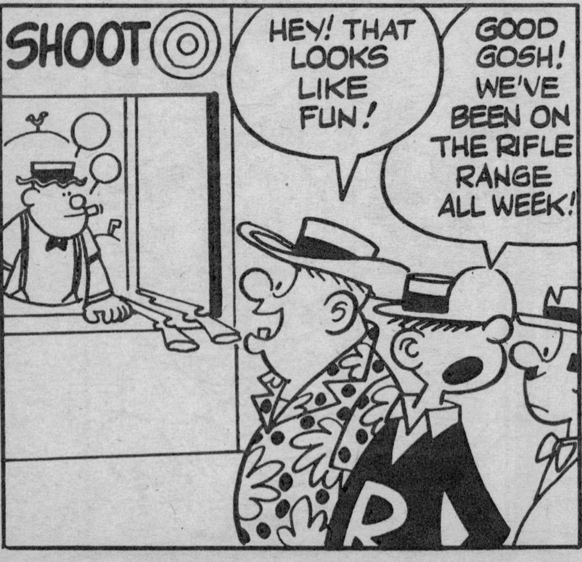
SHOOT
HEY! THAT LOOKS LIKE FUN!
GOOD GOSH! WE'VE BEEN ON THE RIFLE RANGE ALL WEEK!

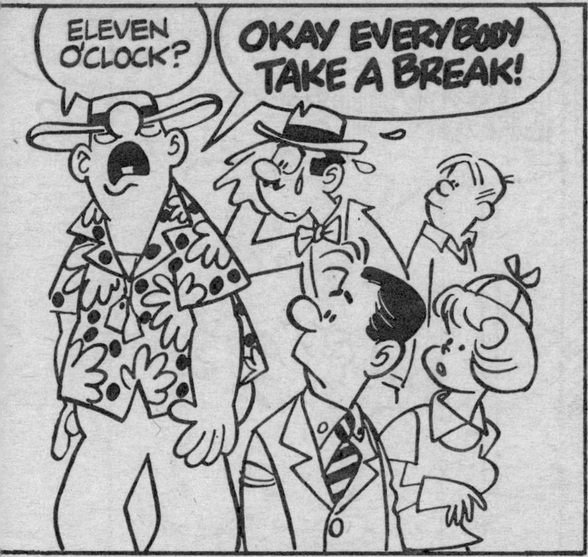
ELEVEN O'CLOCK?
OKAY EVERYBODY TAKE A BREAK!

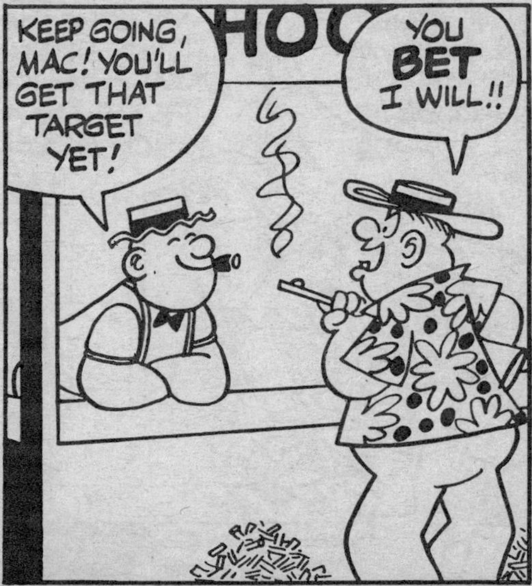
KEEP GOING, MAC! YOU'LL GET THAT TARGET YET!
YOU BET I WILL!!

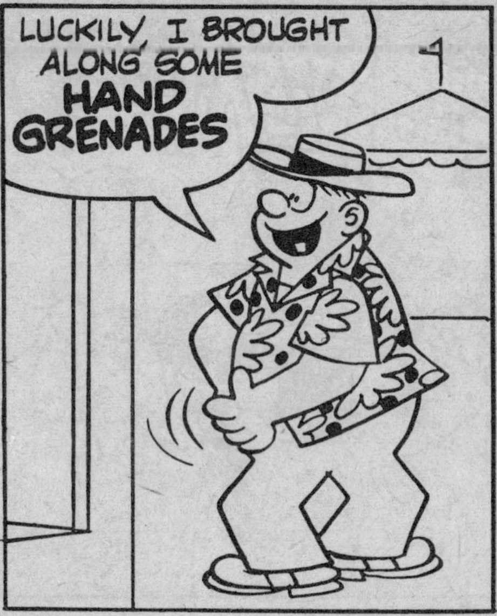
LUCKILY, I BROUGHT ALONG SOME HAND GRENADES

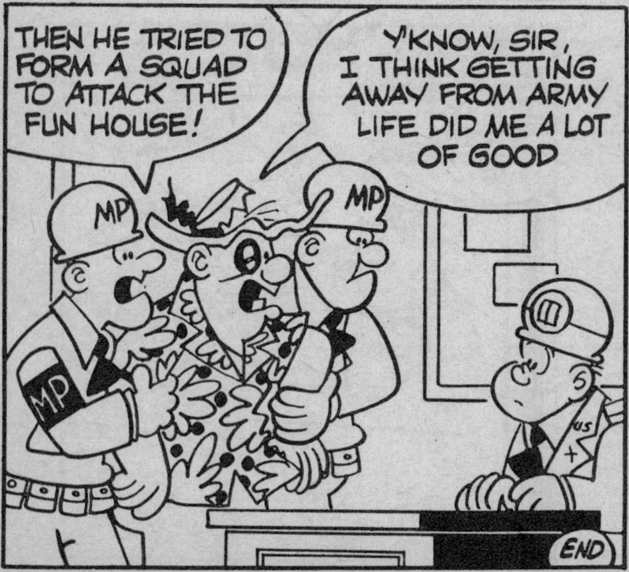
THEN HE TRIED TO FORM A SQUAD TO ATTACK THE FUN HOUSE!
Y'KNOW, SIR, I THINK GETTING AWAY FROM ARMY LIFE DID ME A LOT OF GOOD
MP
MP
MP
US
END

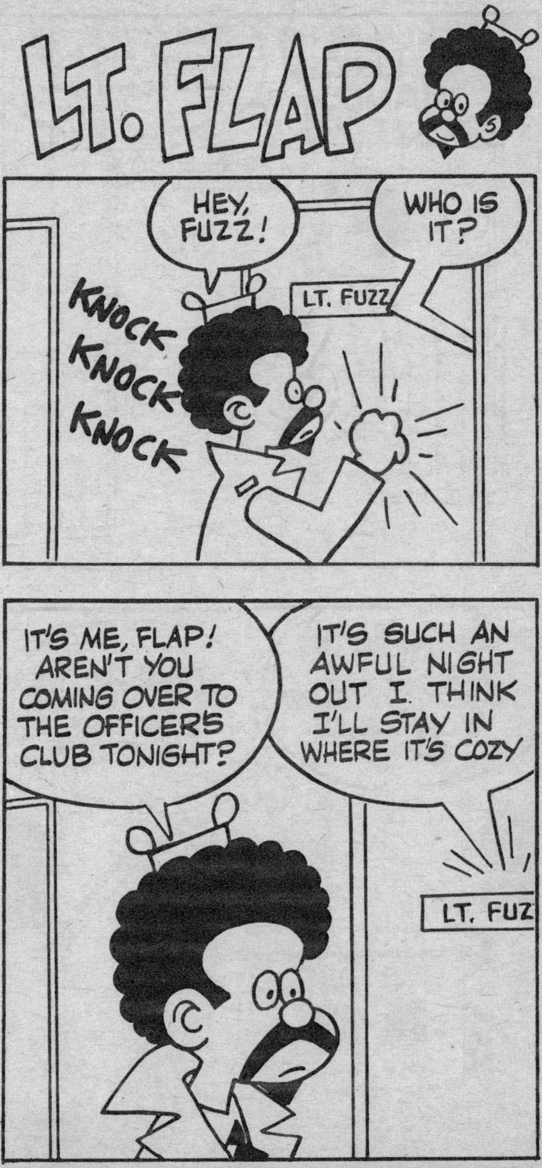
LT. FLAP
HEY, FUZZ!
WHO IS IT?
LT. FUZZ
KNOCK
KNOCK
KNOCK
IT'S ME, FLAP! AREN'T YOU COMING OVER TO THE OFFICER'S CLUB TONIGHT?
IT'S SUCH AN AWFUL NIGHT OUT I. THINK I'LL STAY IN WHERE IT'S COZY
LT. FUZ

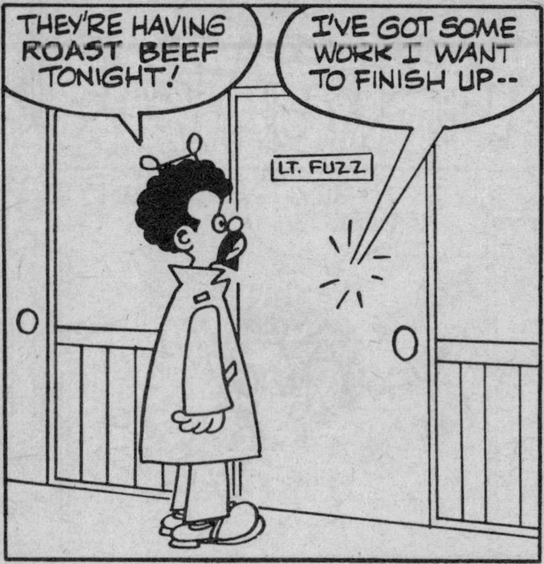
THEY'RE HAVING ROAST BEEF TONIGHT!
I'VE GOT SOME WORK I WANT TO FINISH UP--
LT. FUZZ

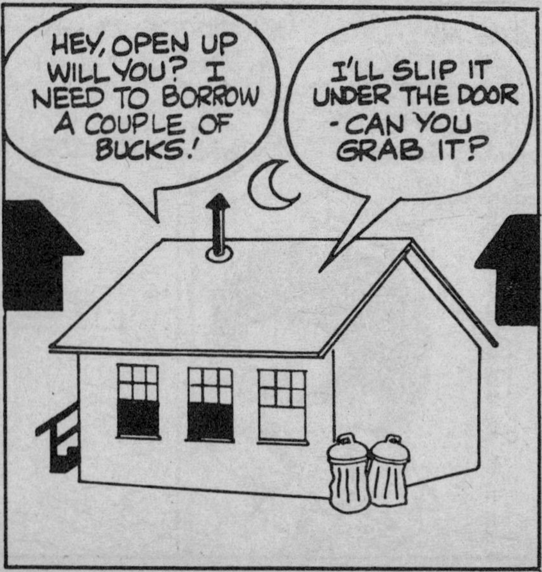
HEY, OPEN UP WILL YOU? I NEED TO BORROW A COUPLE OF BUCKS!
I'LL SLIP IT UNDER THE DOOR - CAN YOU GRAB IT?

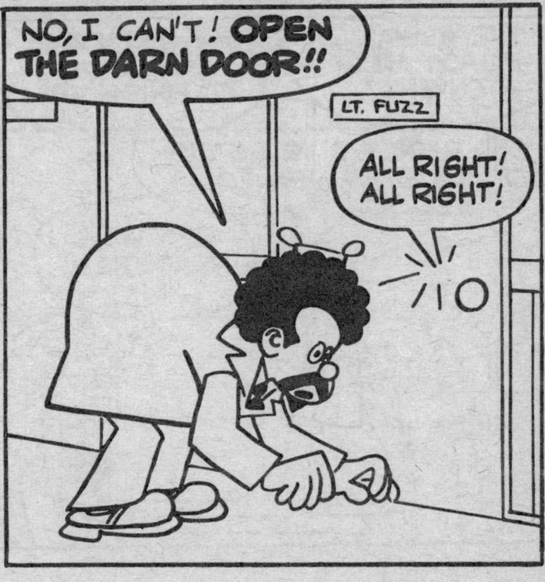
NO, I CAN'T! **OPEN THE DARN DOOR!!**
LT. FUZZ
ALL RIGHT! ALL RIGHT!

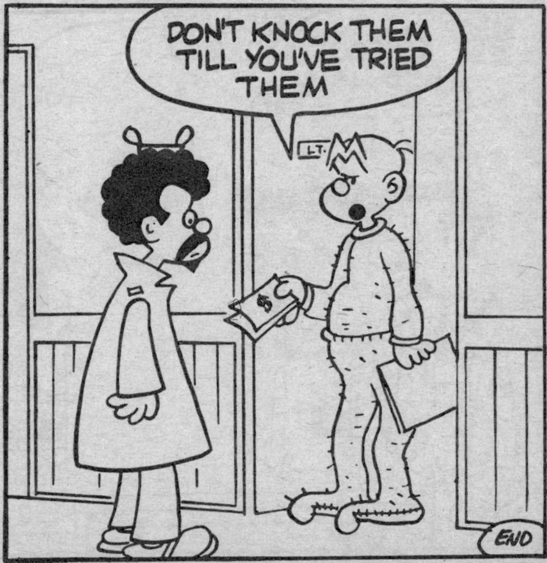
DON'T KNOCK THEM TILL YOU'VE TRIED THEM
LT.
END

"The LISTENER"

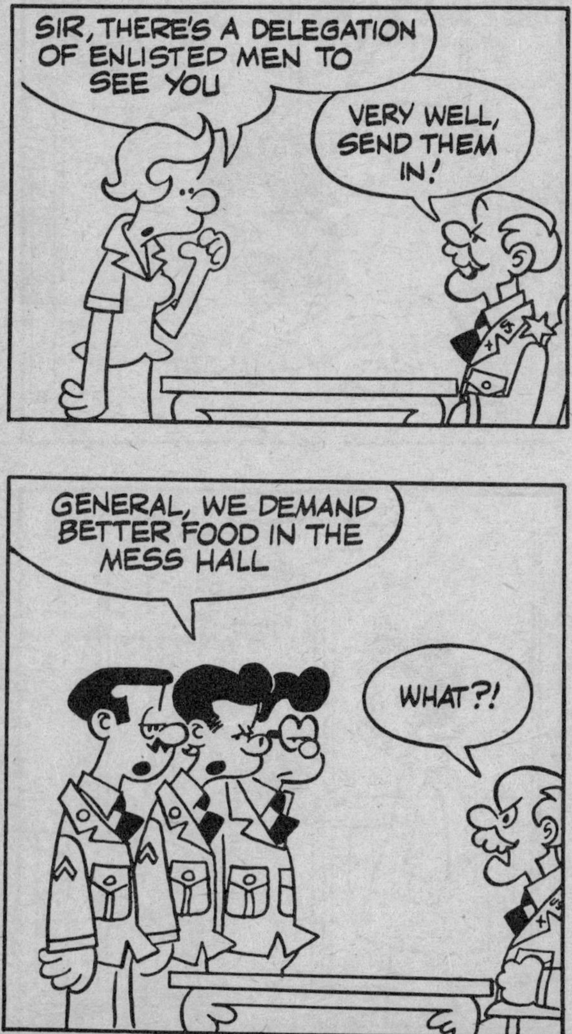
SIR, THERE'S A DELEGATION OF ENLISTED MEN TO SEE YOU
VERY WELL, SEND THEM IN!
GENERAL, WE DEMAND BETTER FOOD IN THE MESS HALL
WHAT?!

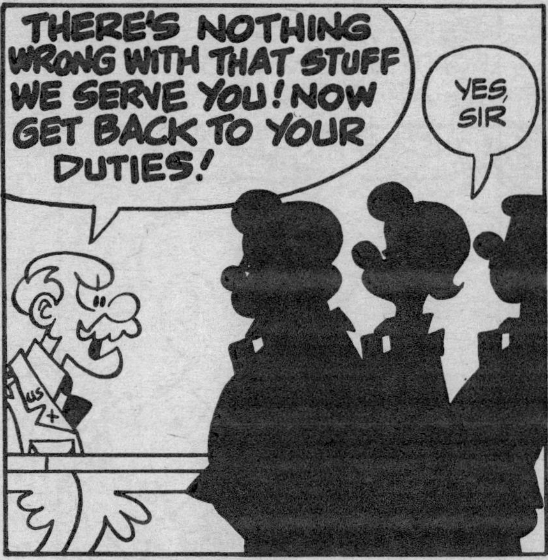
THERE'S NOTHING WRONG WITH THAT STUFF WE SERVE YOU! NOW GET BACK TO YOUR DUTIES!
YES, SIR
US

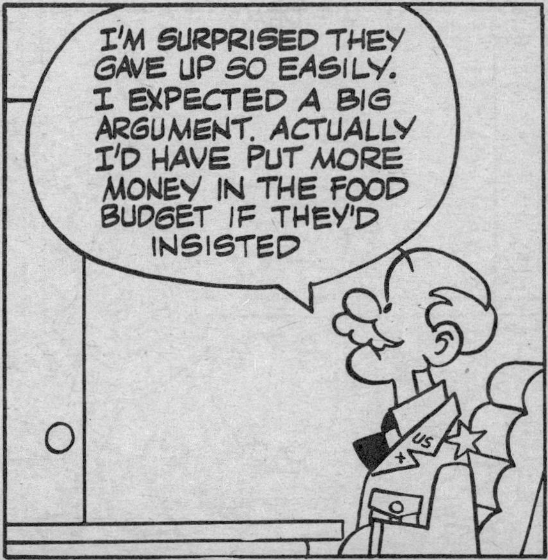
I'M SURPRISED THEY GAVE UP SO EASILY. I EXPECTED A BIG ARGUMENT. ACTUALLY I'D HAVE PUT MORE MONEY IN THE FOOD BUDGET IF THEY'D INSISTED
US

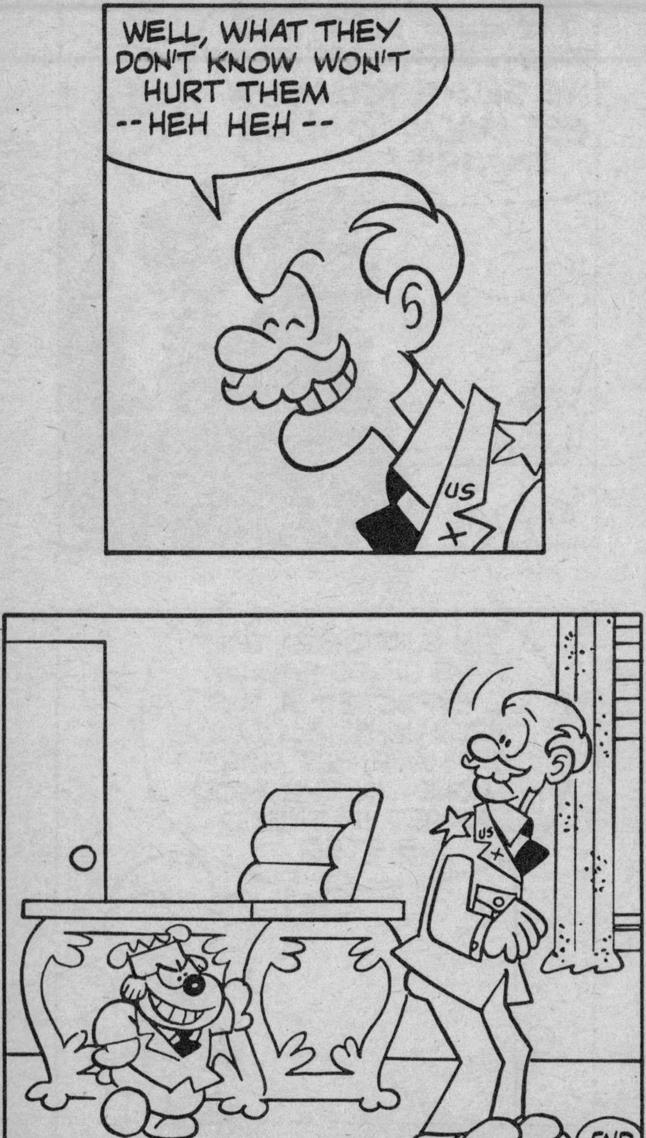
WELL, WHAT THEY DON'T KNOW WON'T HURT THEM --HEH HEH --
US
US
END

The
CAMOUFLAGE
CLASS

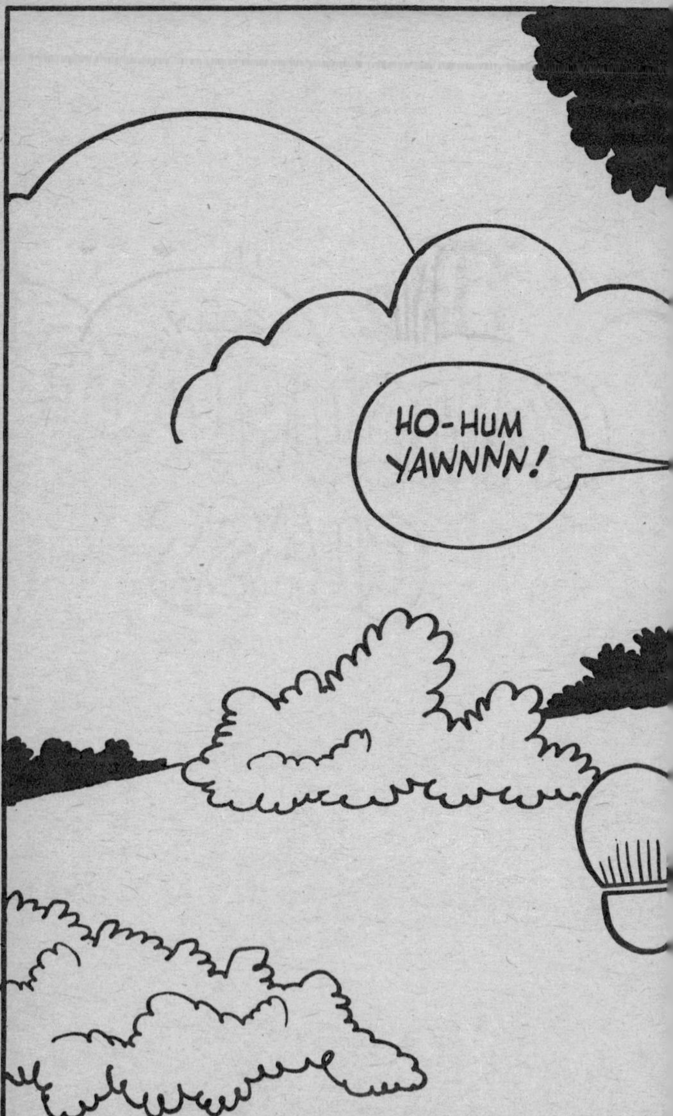
HO-HUM YAWNNN!

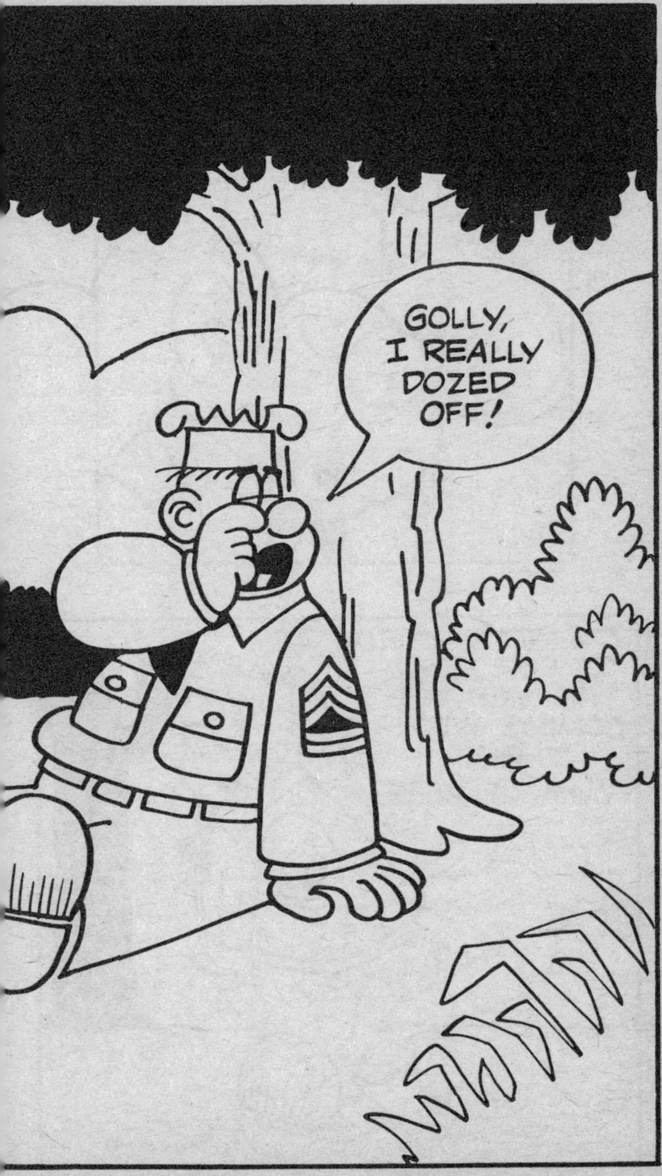
GOLLY, I REALLY DOZED OFF!

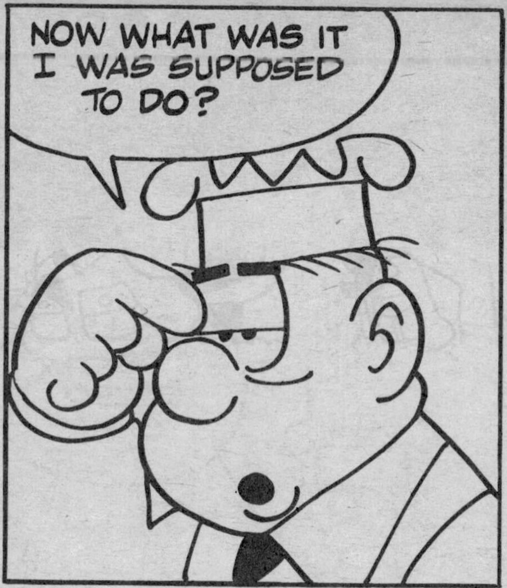
NOW WHAT WAS IT I WAS SUPPOSED TO DO?

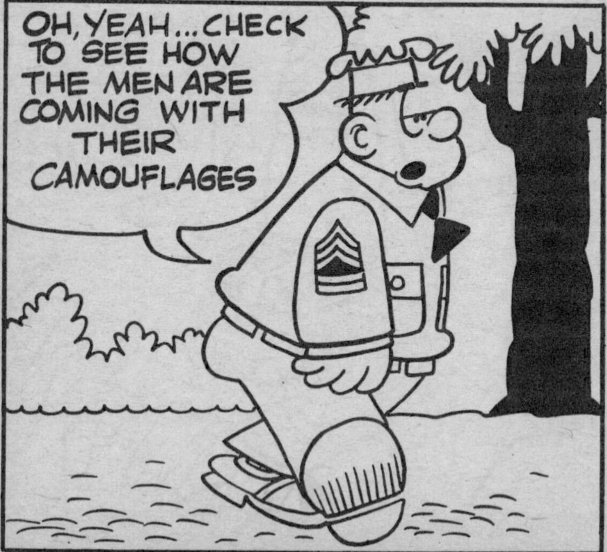
OH, YEAH...CHECK TO SEE HOW THE MEN ARE COMING WITH THEIR CAMOUFLAGES

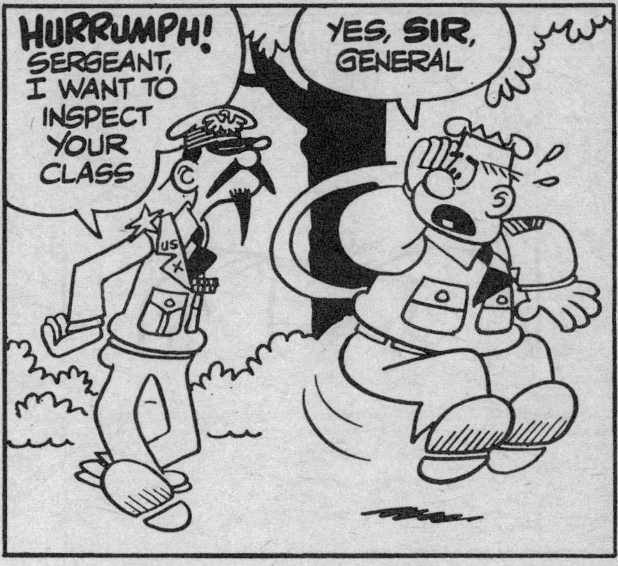
HURRUMPH! SERGEANT, I WANT TO INSPECT YOUR CLASS
YES, SIR, GENERAL

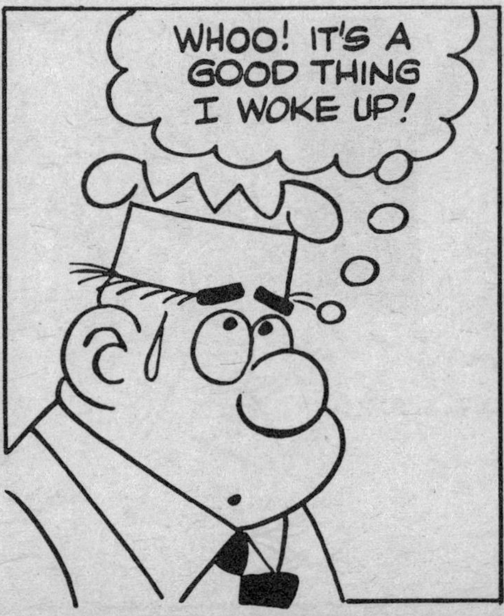
WHOO! IT'S A GOOD THING I WOKE UP!

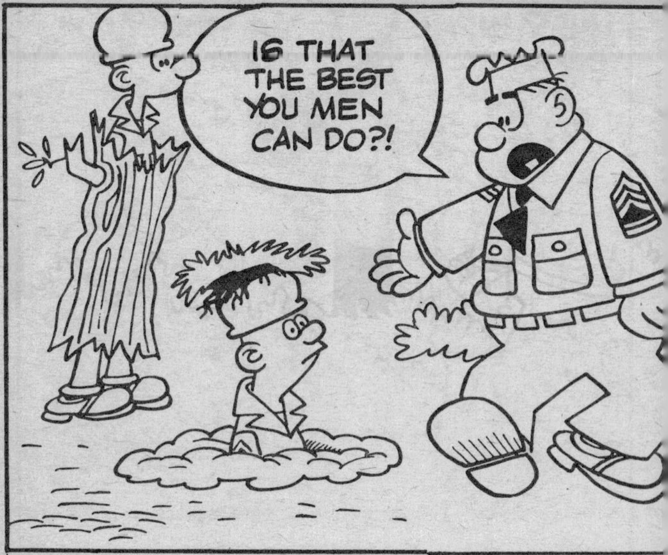
IS THAT THE BEST YOU MEN CAN DO?!

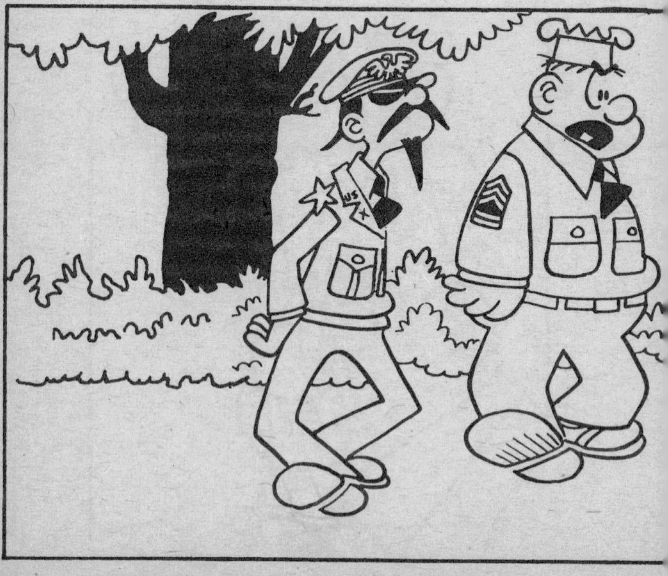

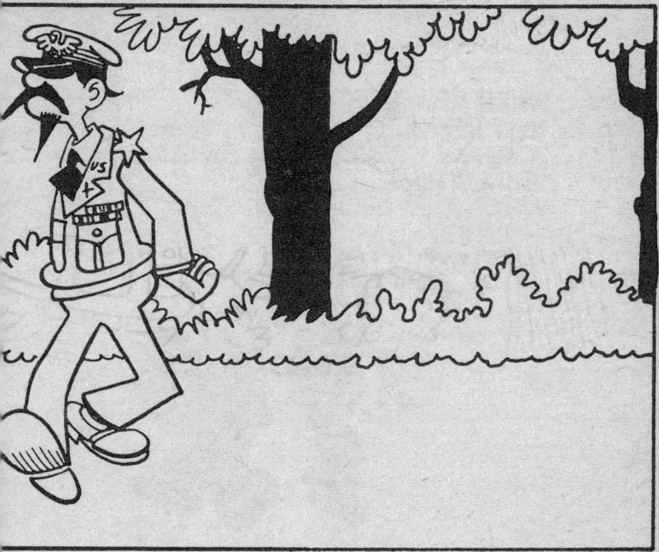

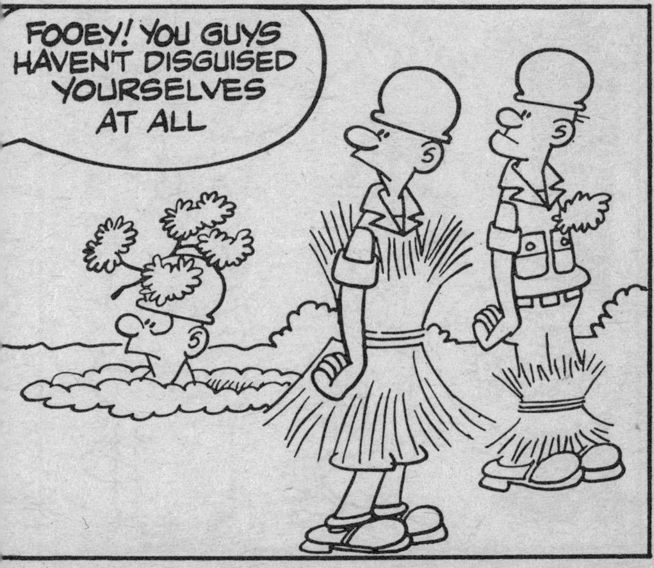
FOOEY! YOU GUYS HAVEN'T DISGUISED YOURSELVES AT ALL

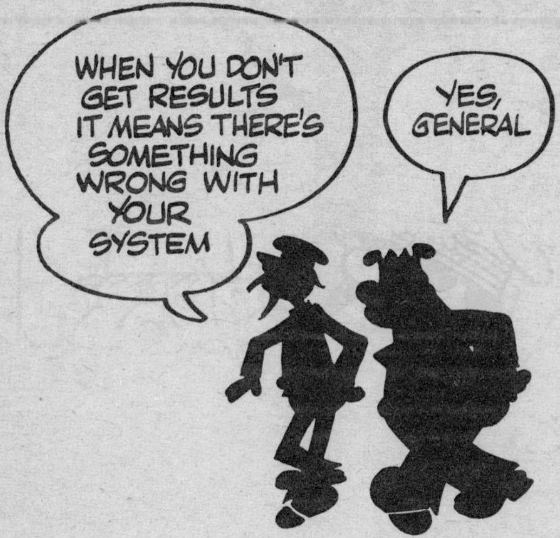
WHEN YOU DON'T GET RESULTS IT MEANS THERE'S SOMETHING WRONG WITH YOUR SYSTEM
YES, GENERAL

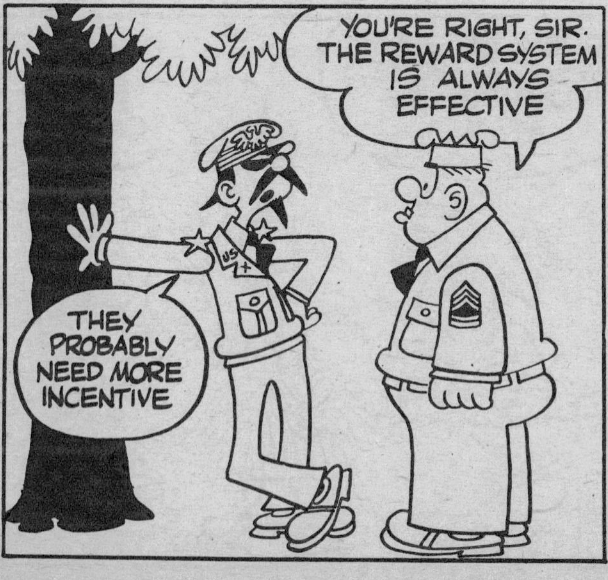
THEY PROBABLY NEED MORE INCENTIVE
YOU'RE RIGHT, SIR. THE REWARD SYSTEM IS ALWAYS EFFECTIVE

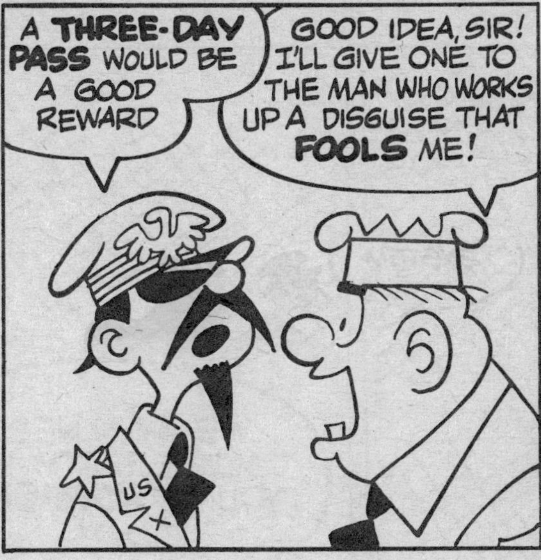
A **THREE-DAY PASS** WOULD BE A GOOD REWARD
GOOD IDEA, SIR! I'LL GIVE ONE TO THE MAN WHO WORKS UP A DISGUISE THAT **FOOLS** ME!
US

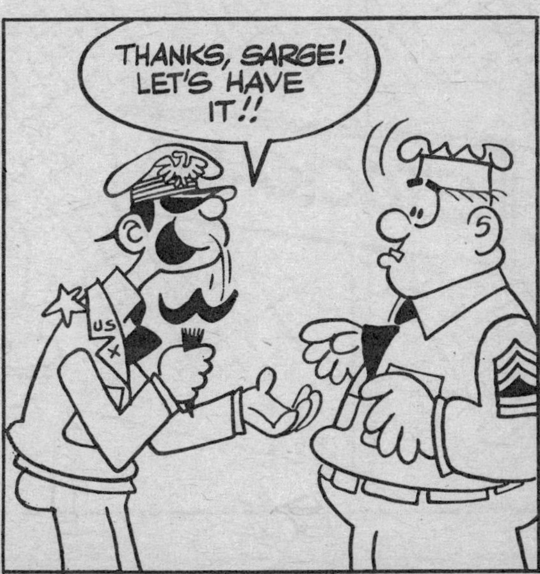
THANKS, SARGE! LET'S HAVE IT!!
US

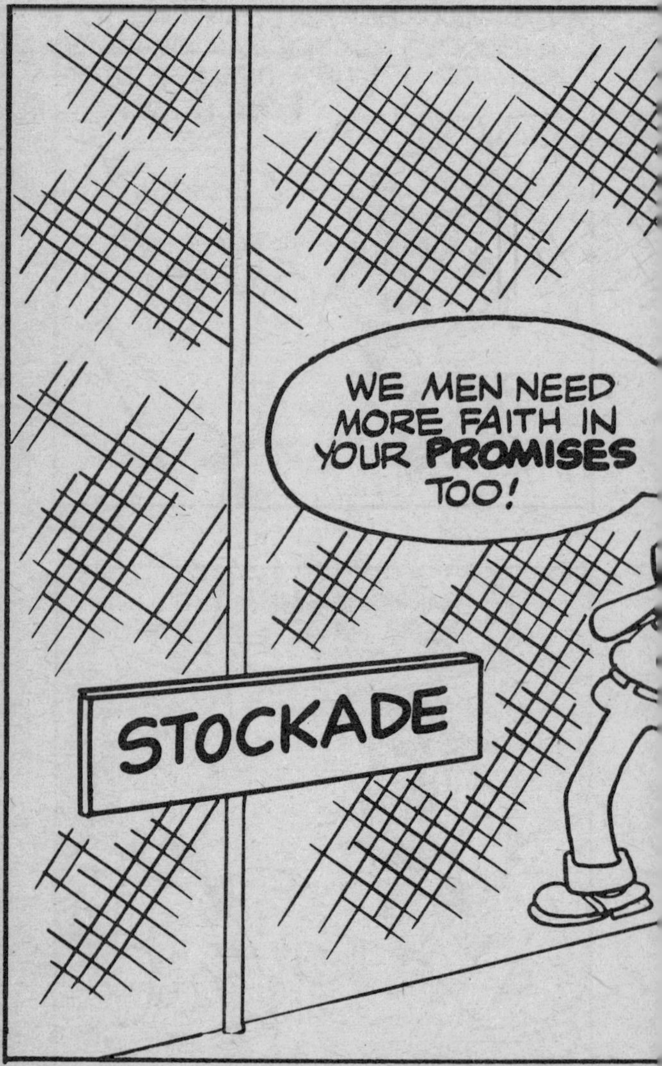
WE MEN NEED MORE FAITH IN YOUR PROMISES TOO!
STOCKADE

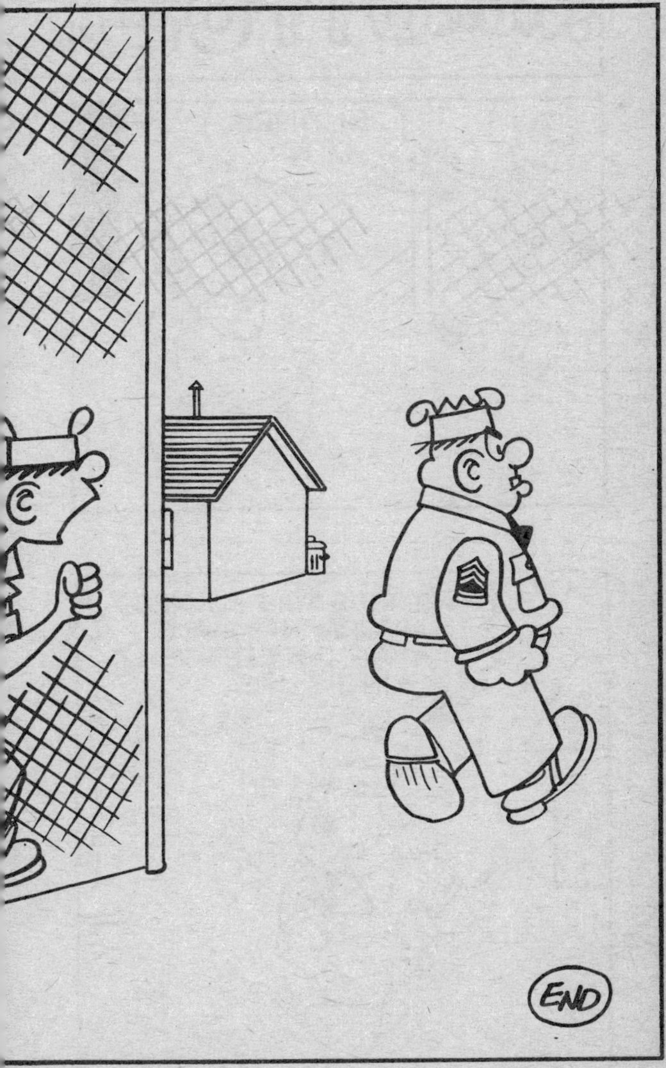
END

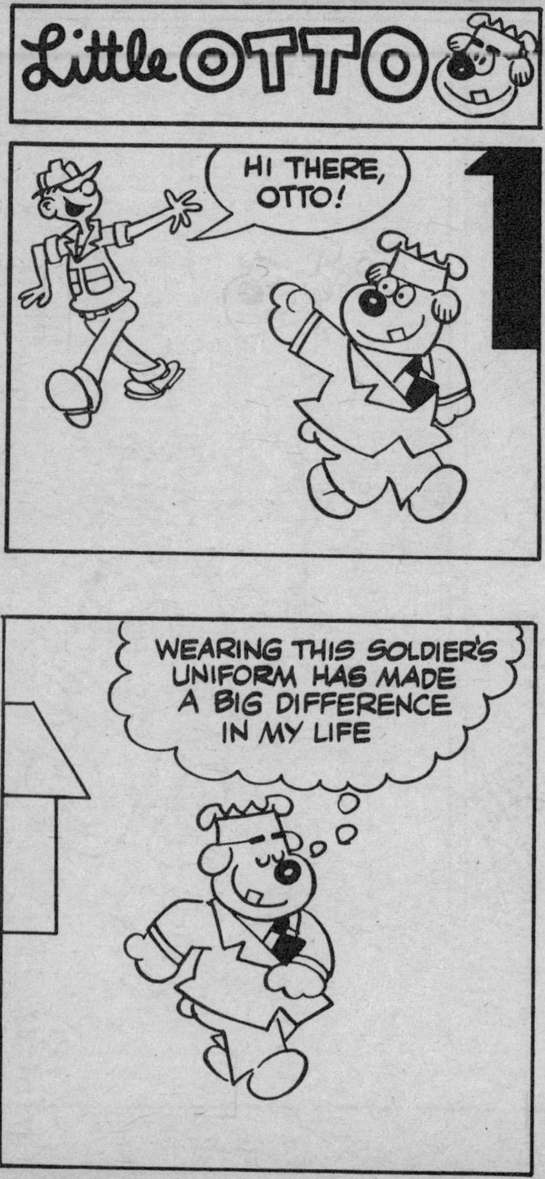
Little OTTO
1
HI THERE, OTTO!
WEARING THIS SOLDIER'S UNIFORM HAS MADE A BIG DIFFERENCE IN MY LIFE

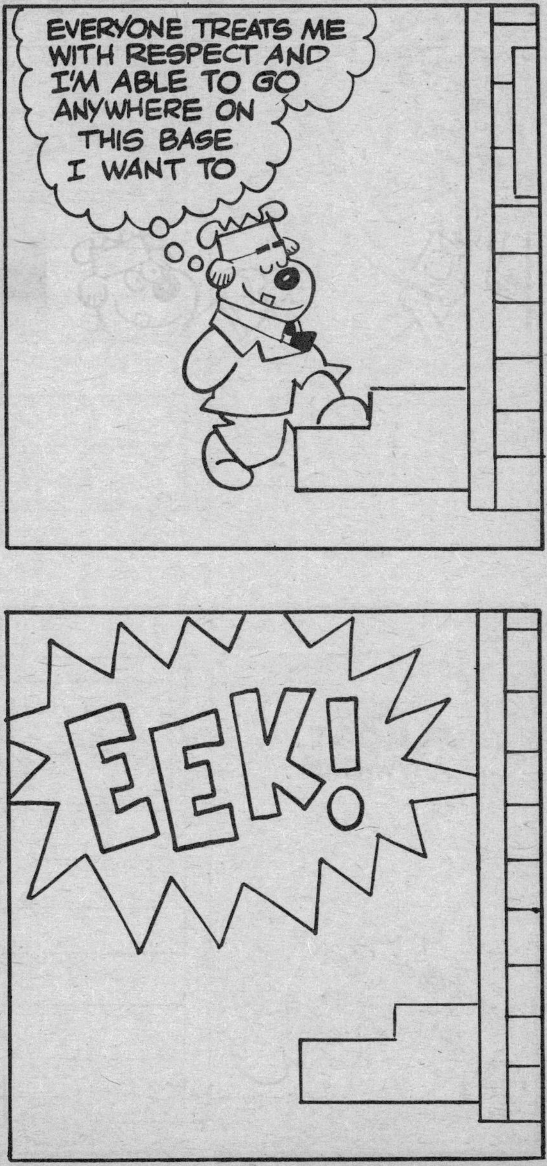
EVERYONE TREATS ME WITH RESPECT AND I'M ABLE TO GO ANYWHERE ON THIS BASE I WANT TO
EEK!

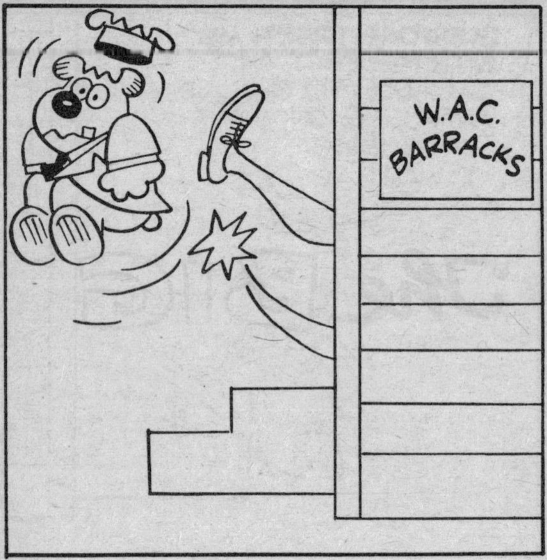
W.A.C.
BARRACKS

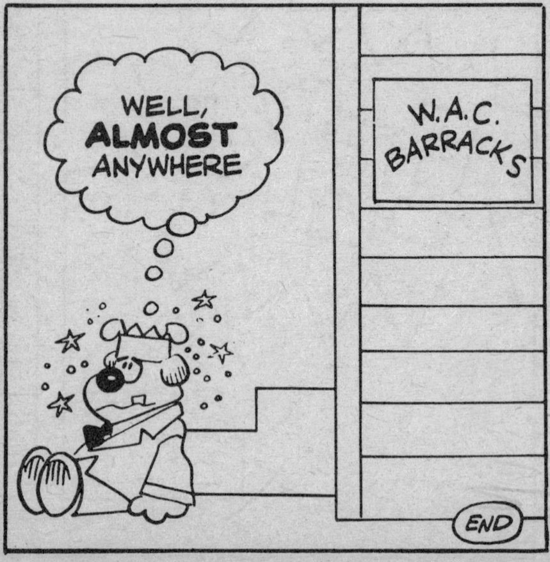
WELL, **ALMOST** ANYWHERE
W.A.C.
BARRACKS
END

The BIG SPLASH

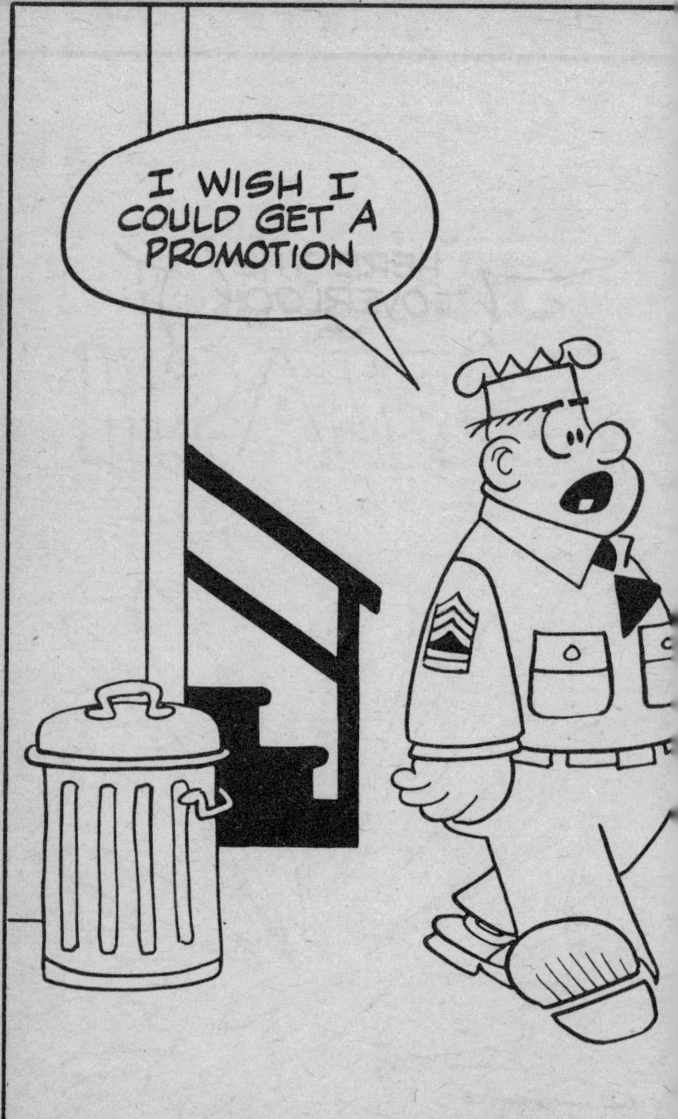
I WISH I COULD GET A PROMOTION

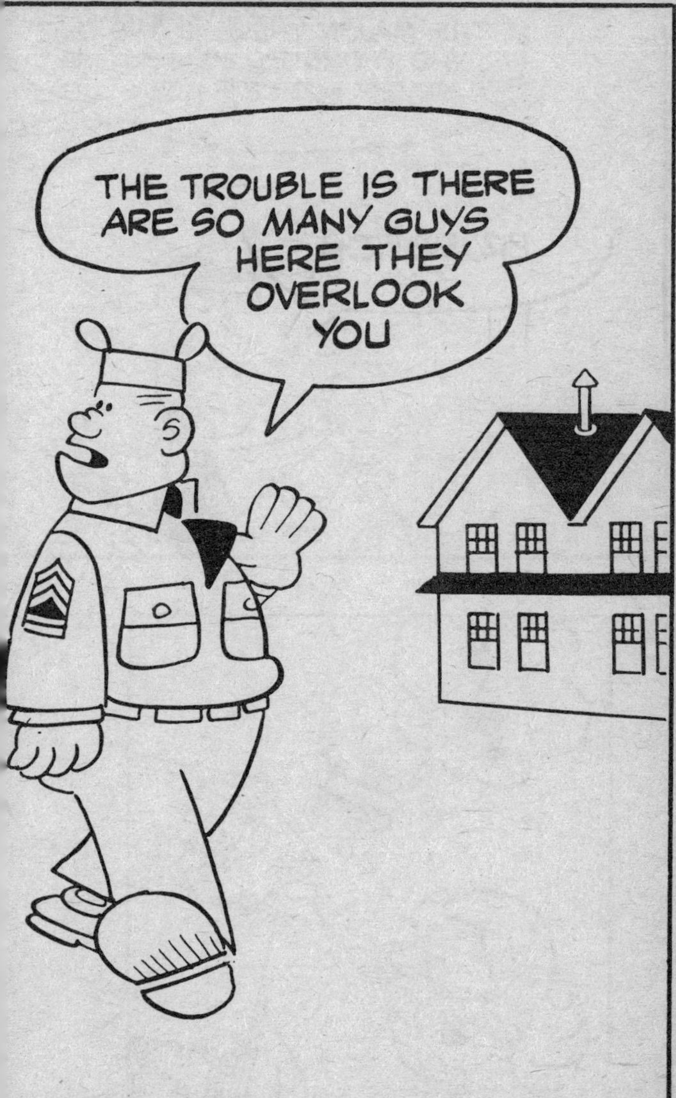
THE TROUBLE IS THERE ARE SO MANY GUYS HERE THEY OVERLOOK YOU

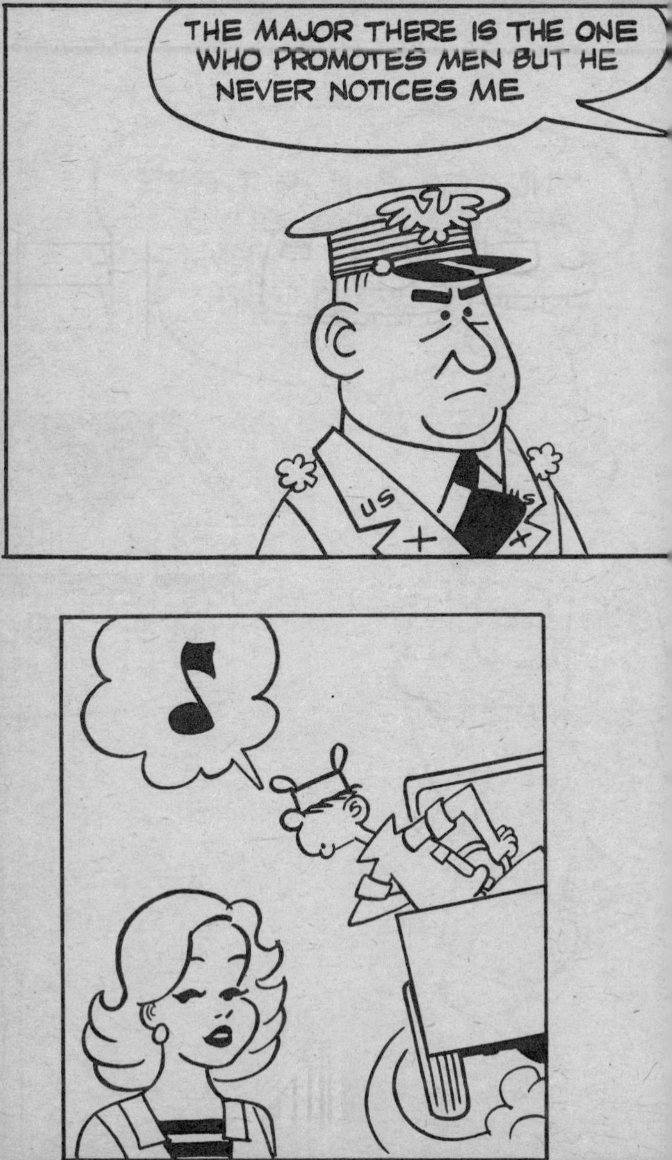
THE MAJOR THERE IS THE ONE WHO PROMOTES MEN BUT HE NEVER NOTICES ME.

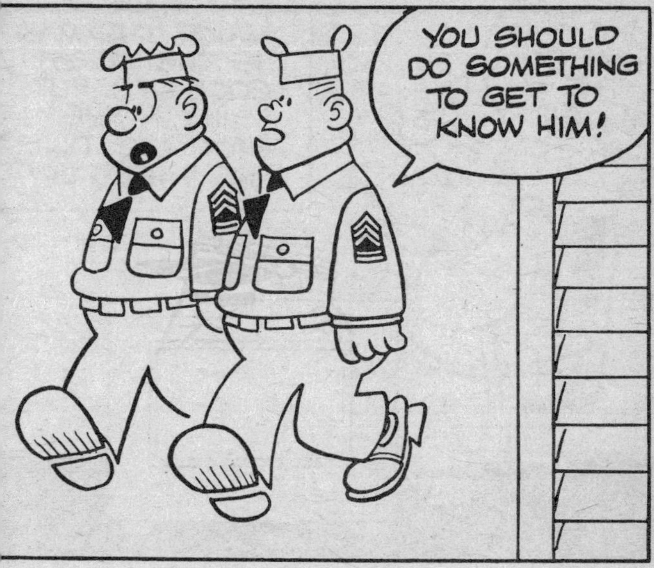
YOU SHOULD DO SOMETHING TO GET TO KNOW HIM!

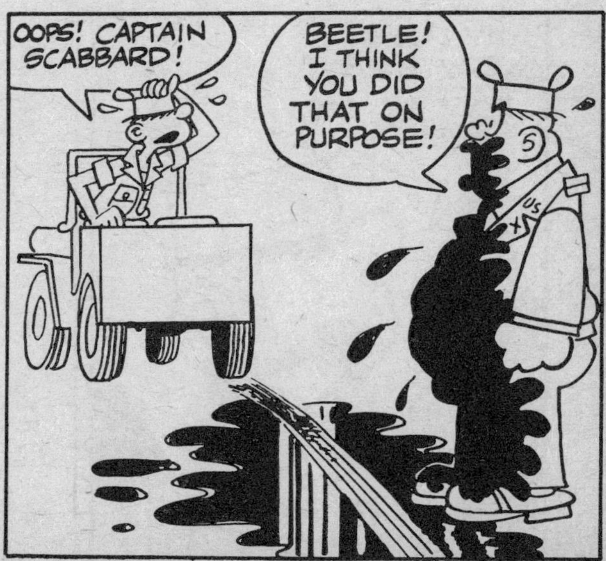
OOPS! CAPTAIN SCABBARD!
BEETLE! I THINK YOU DID THAT ON PURPOSE!

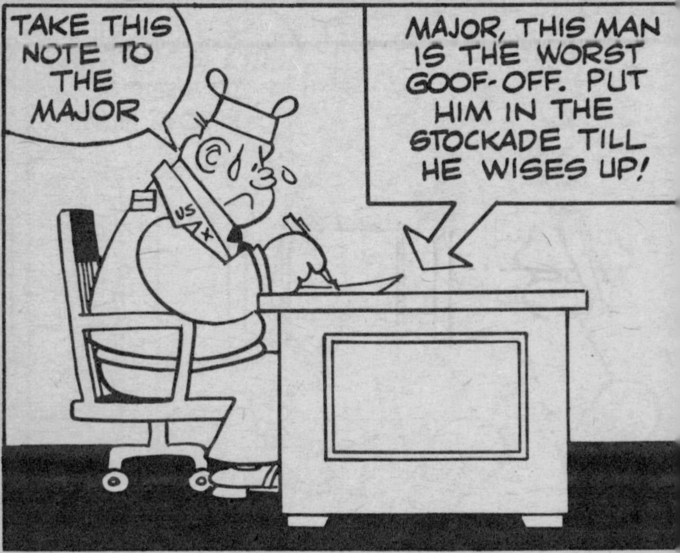
TAKE THIS NOTE TO THE MAJOR
MAJOR, THIS MAN IS THE WORST GOOF-OFF. PUT HIM IN THE STOCKADE TILL HE WISES UP!

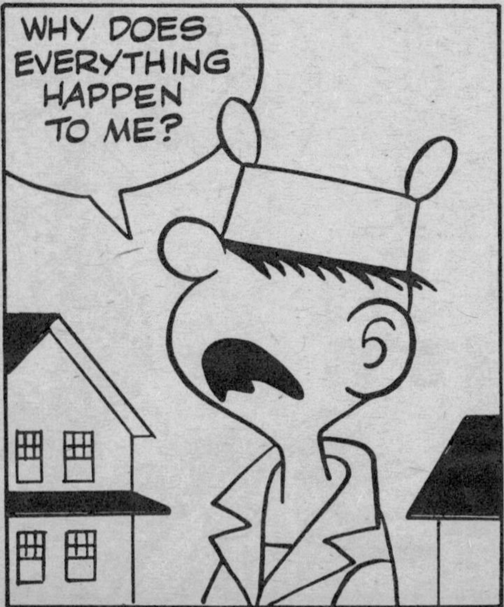
WHY DOES EVERYTHING HAPPEN TO ME?

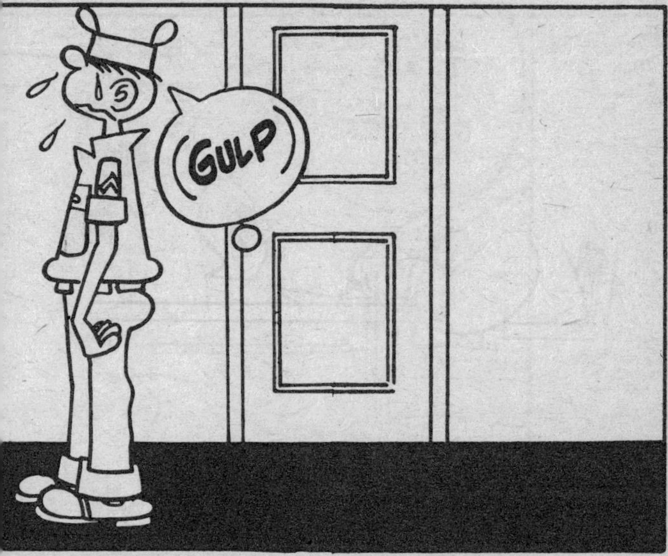
GULP

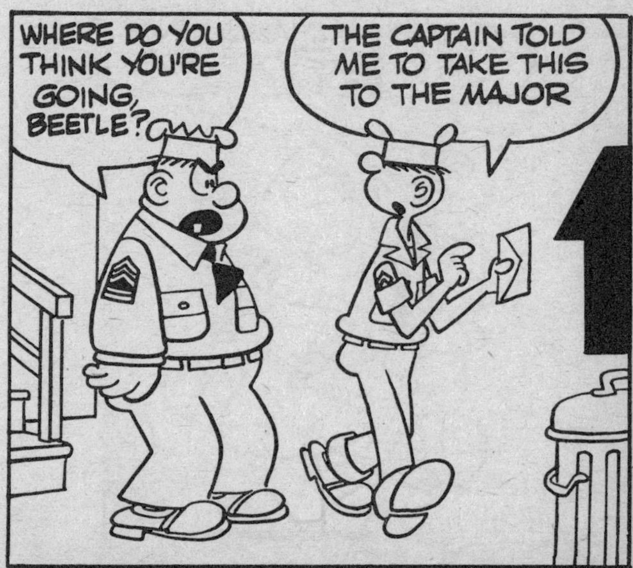
WHERE DO YOU THINK YOU'RE GOING, BEETLE?
THE CAPTAIN TOLD ME TO TAKE THIS TO THE MAJOR

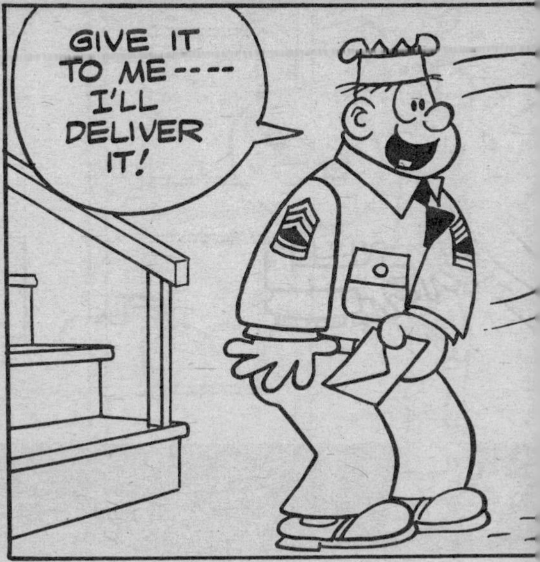
GIVE IT TO ME---- I'LL DELIVER IT!

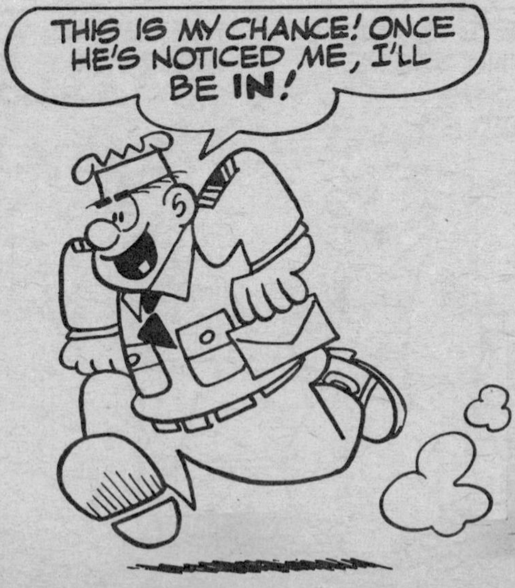
THIS IS MY CHANCE! ONCE HE'S NOTICED ME, I'LL BE **IN**!

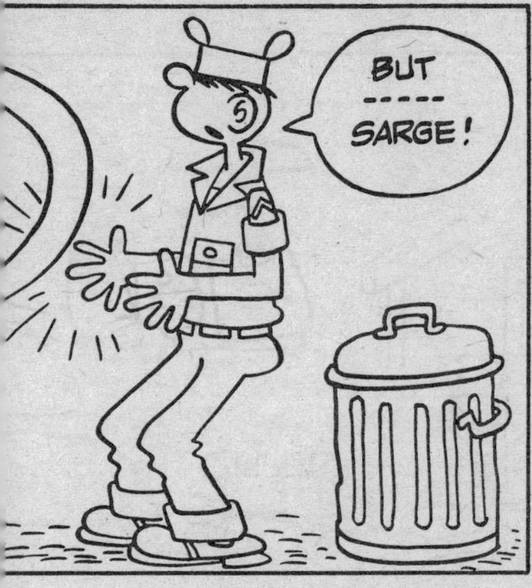
BUT ----- SARGE!

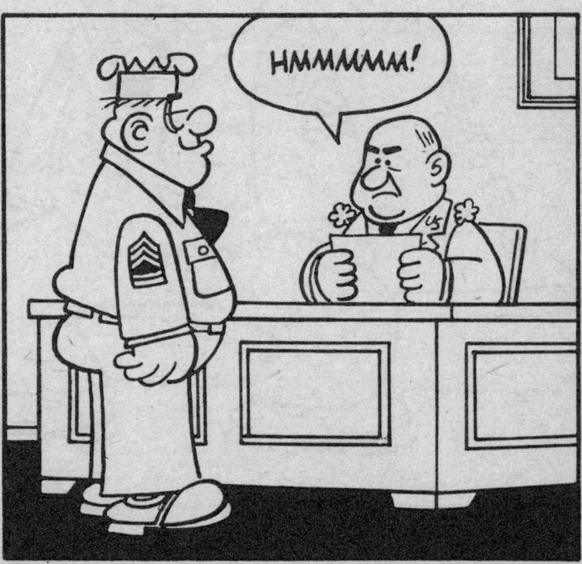
HMMMMM!

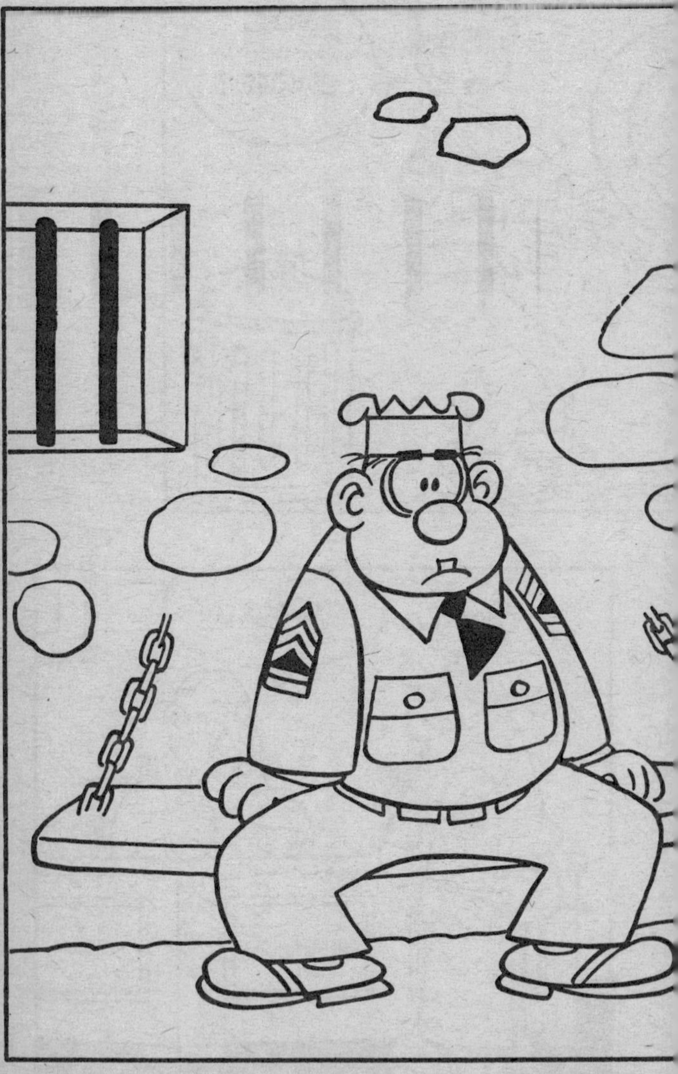

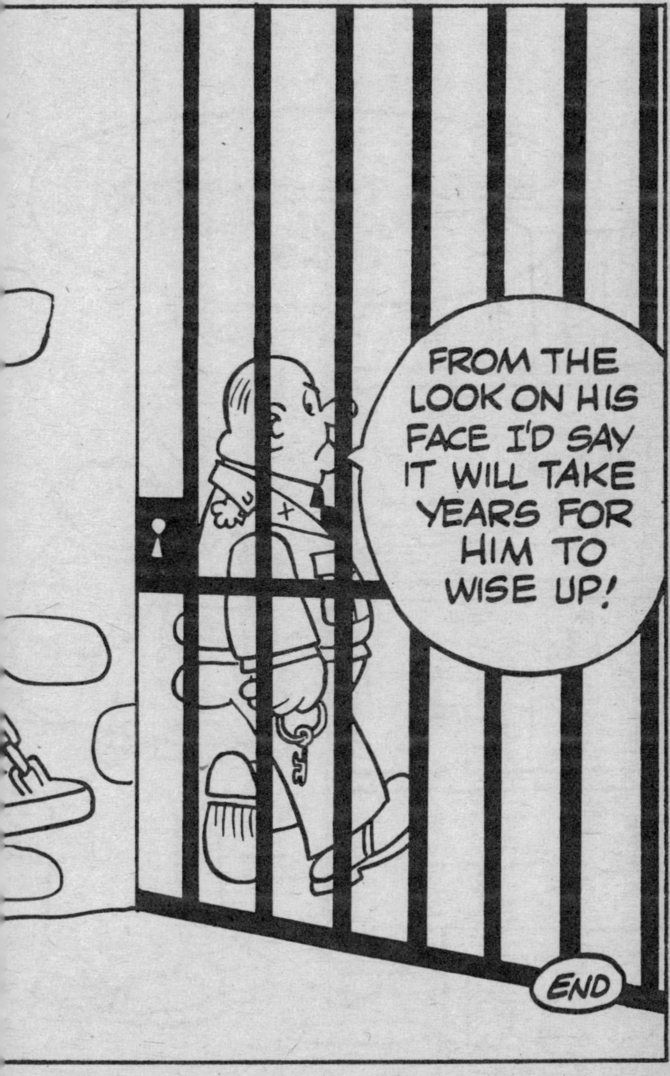
FROM THE LOOK ON HIS FACE I'D SAY IT WILL TAKE YEARS FOR HIM TO WISE UP!
END

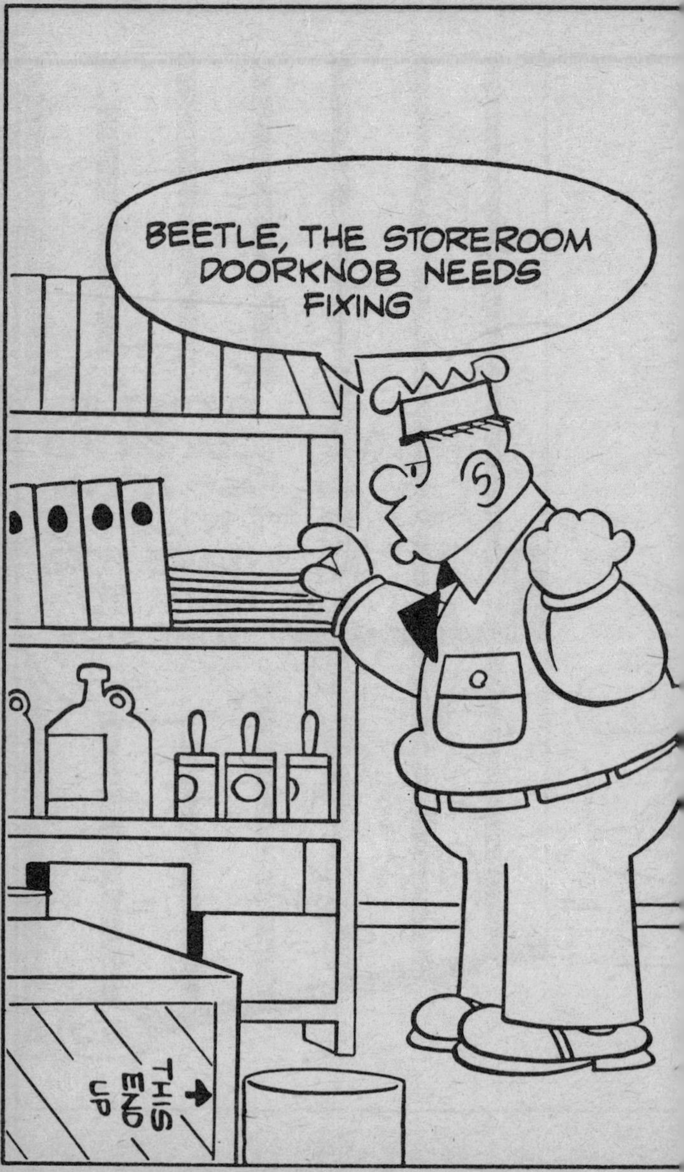
BEETLE, THE STOREROOM DOORKNOB NEEDS FIXING
THIS END UP

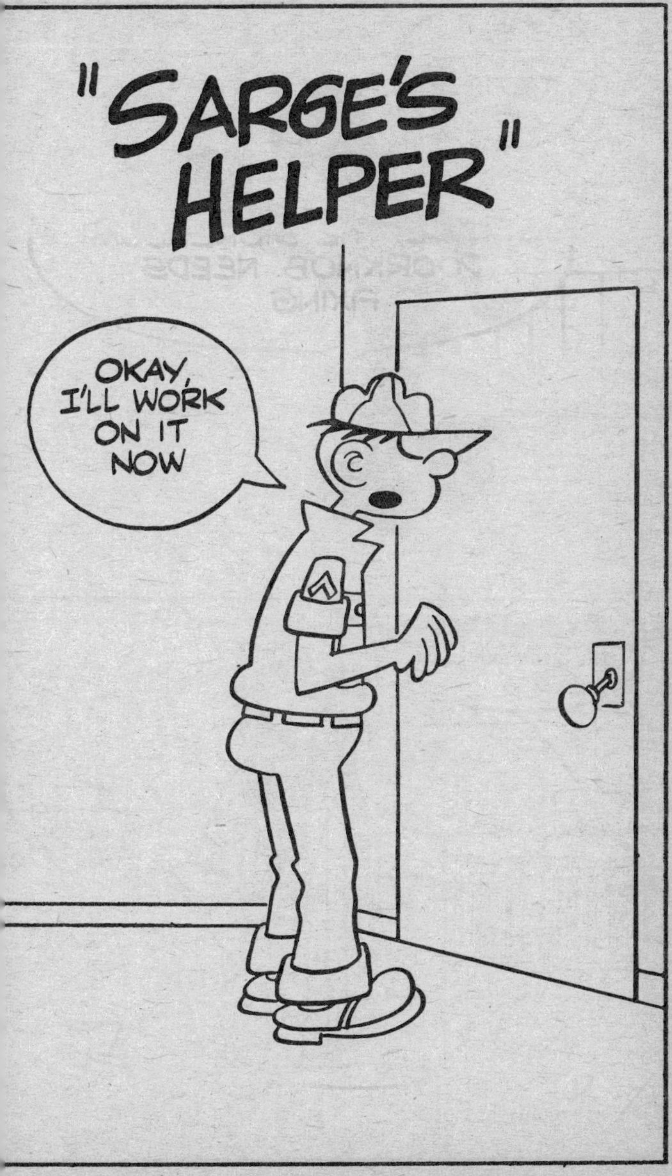
"SARGE'S HELPER"
OKAY, I'LL WORK ON IT NOW

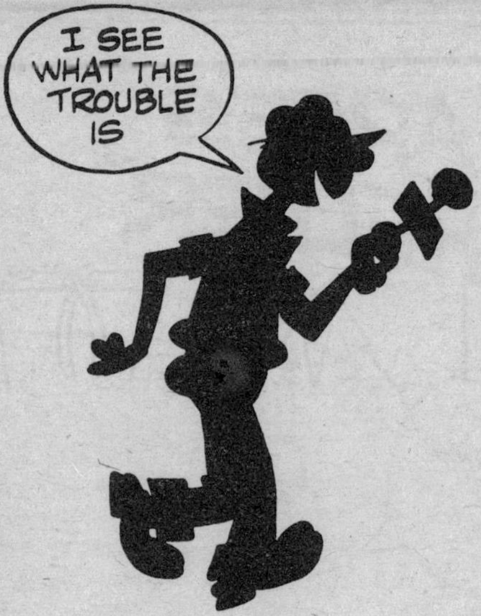
I SEE WHAT THE TROUBLE IS

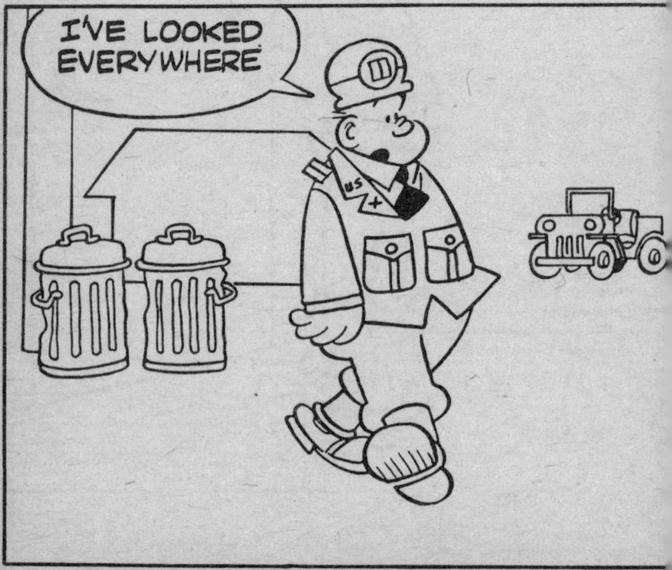
I'VE LOOKED EVERYWHERE

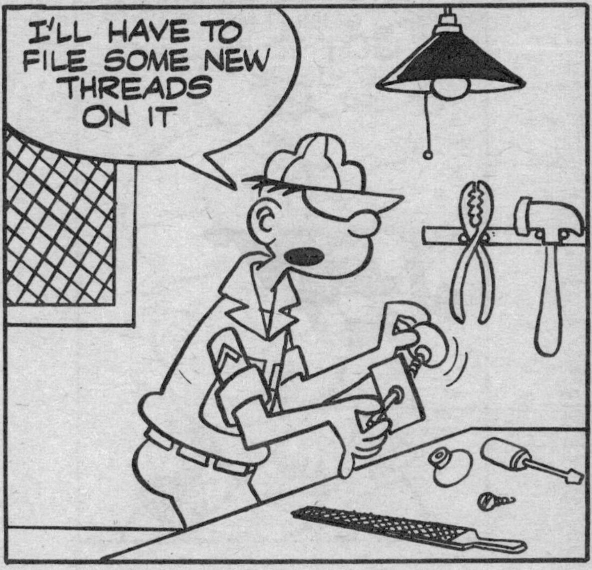
I'LL HAVE TO FILE SOME NEW THREADS ON IT

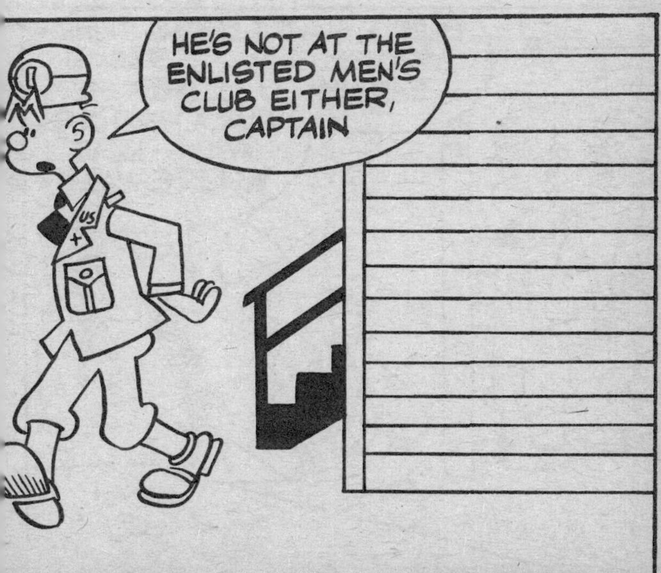
HE'S NOT AT THE ENLISTED MEN'S CLUB EITHER, CAPTAIN

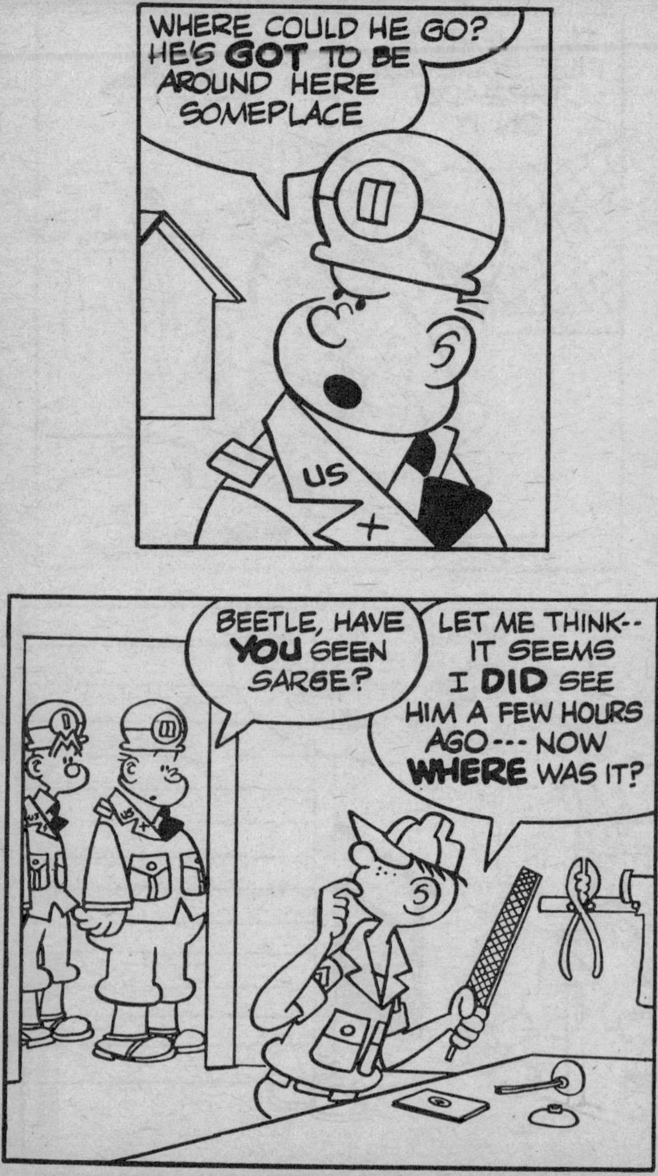
WHERE COULD HE GO? HE'S GOT TO BE AROUND HERE SOMEPLACE
BEETLE, HAVE YOU SEEN SARGE?
LET ME THINK-- IT SEEMS I DID SEE HIM A FEW HOURS AGO--- NOW WHERE WAS IT?

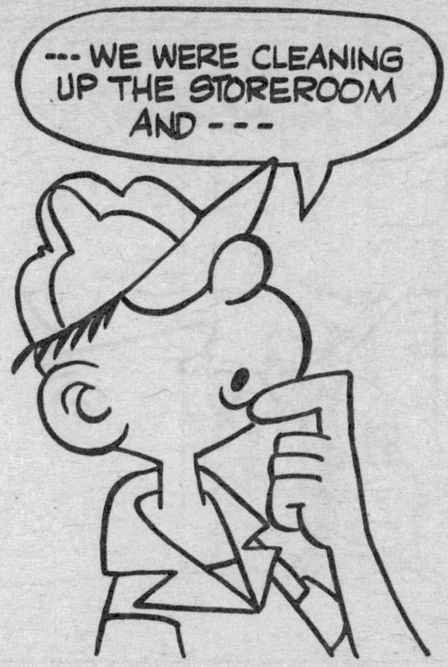
--- WE WERE CLEANING UP THE STOREROOM AND ---

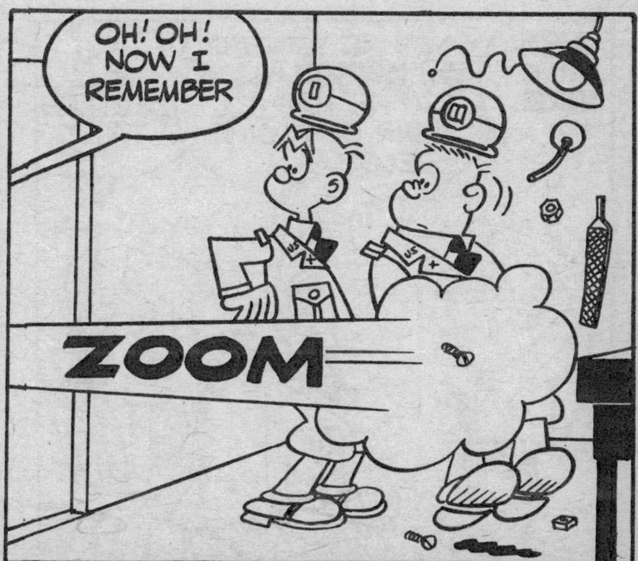
OH! OH! NOW I REMEMBER
ZOOM

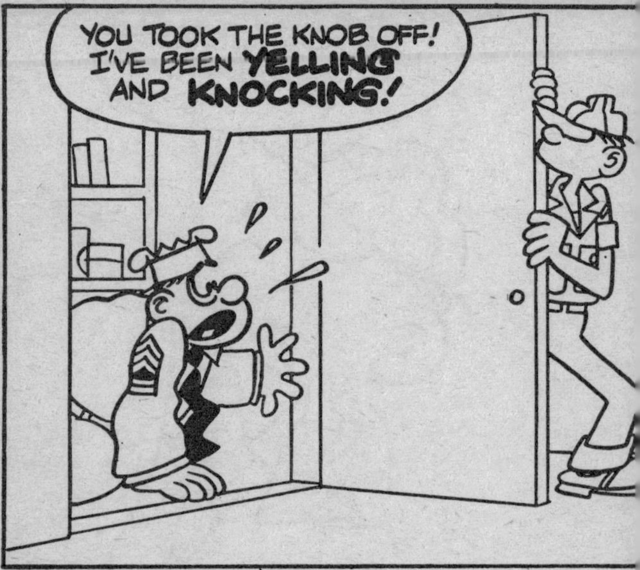
YOU TOOK THE KNOB OFF! I'VE BEEN YELLING AND KNOCKING!

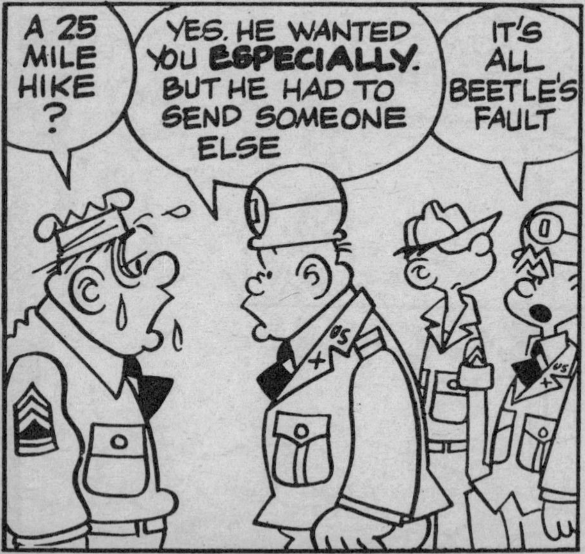
A 25 MILE HIKE ?
YES. HE WANTED YOU ESPECIALLY. BUT HE HAD TO SEND SOMEONE ELSE
IT'S ALL BEETLE'S FAULT

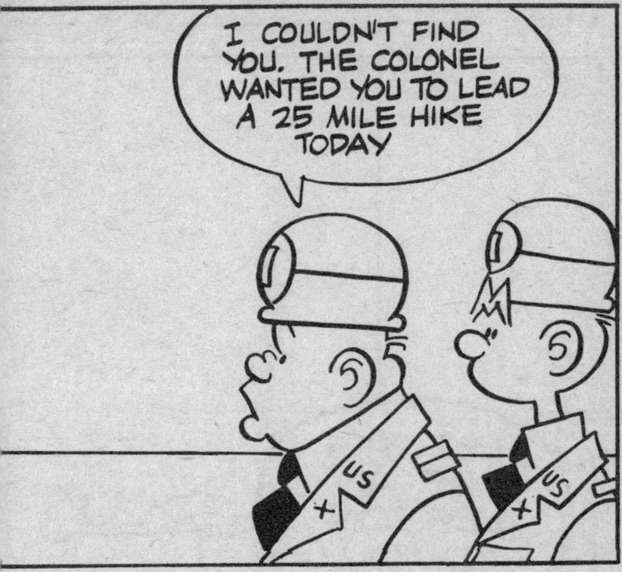
I COULDN'T FIND YOU. THE COLONEL WANTED YOU TO LEAD A 25 MILE HIKE TODAY
US
US

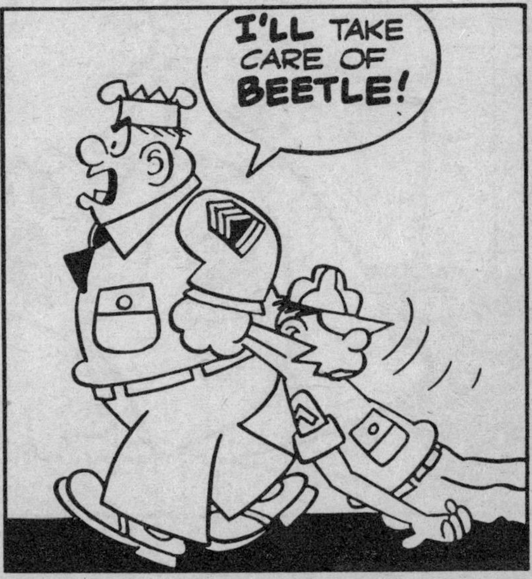
I'LL TAKE CARE OF BEETLE!

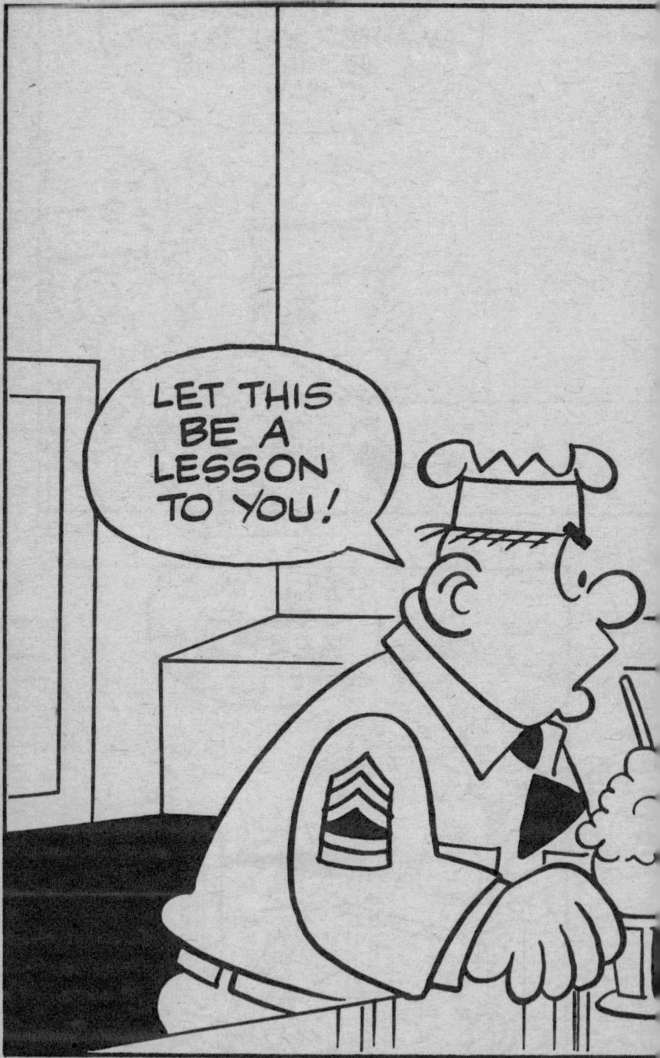
LET THIS BE A LESSON TO YOU!

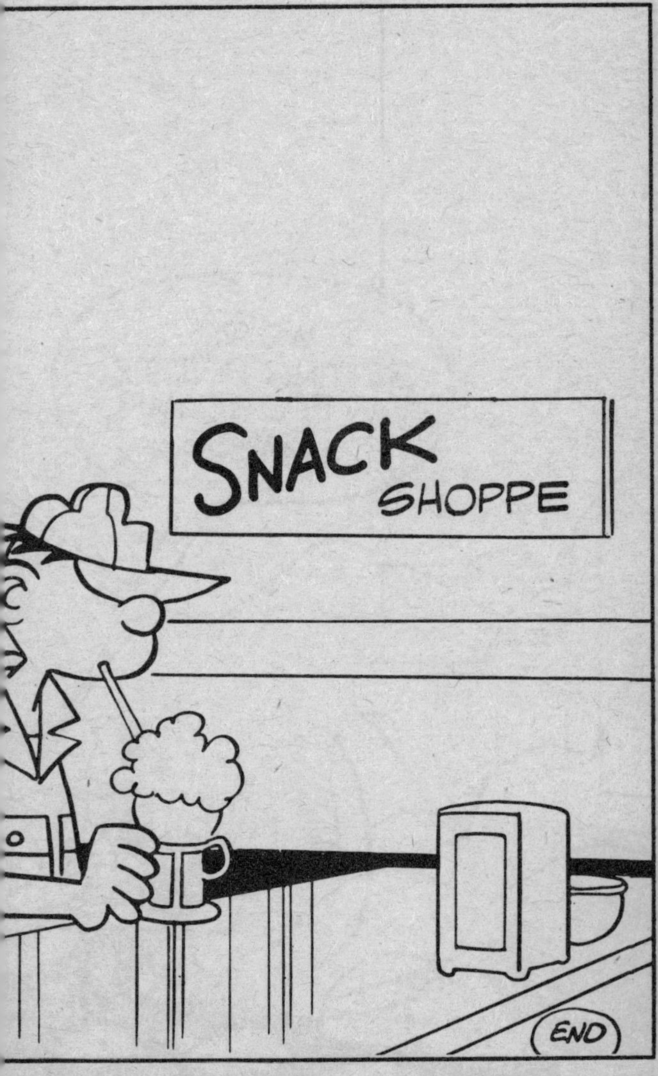
SNACK SHOPPE
END

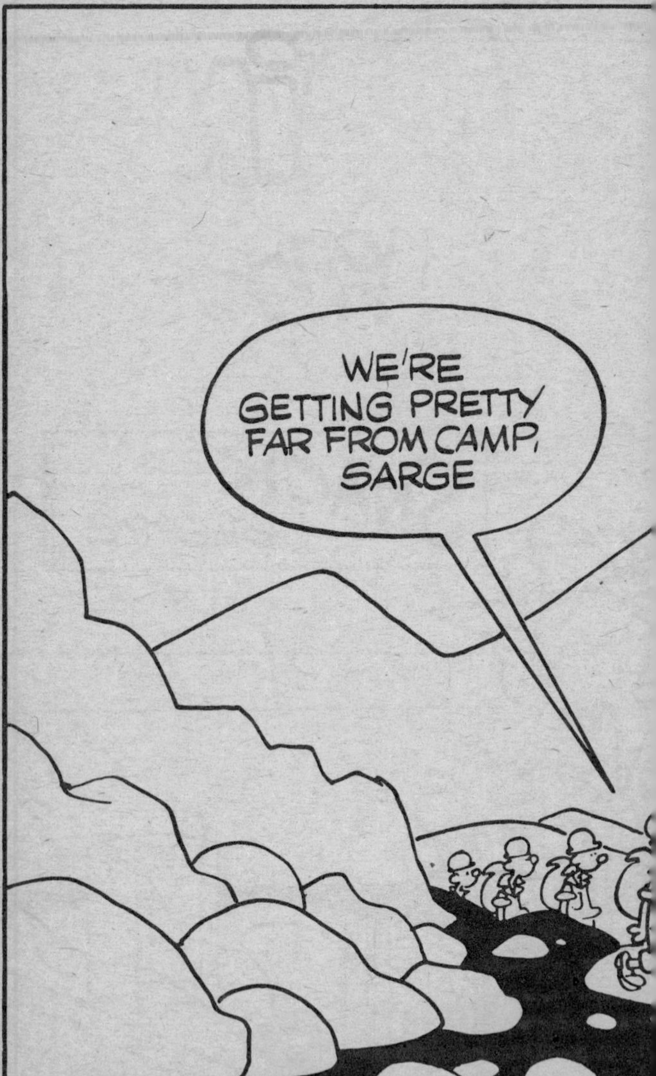
WE'RE GETTING PRETTY FAR FROM CAMP, SARGE

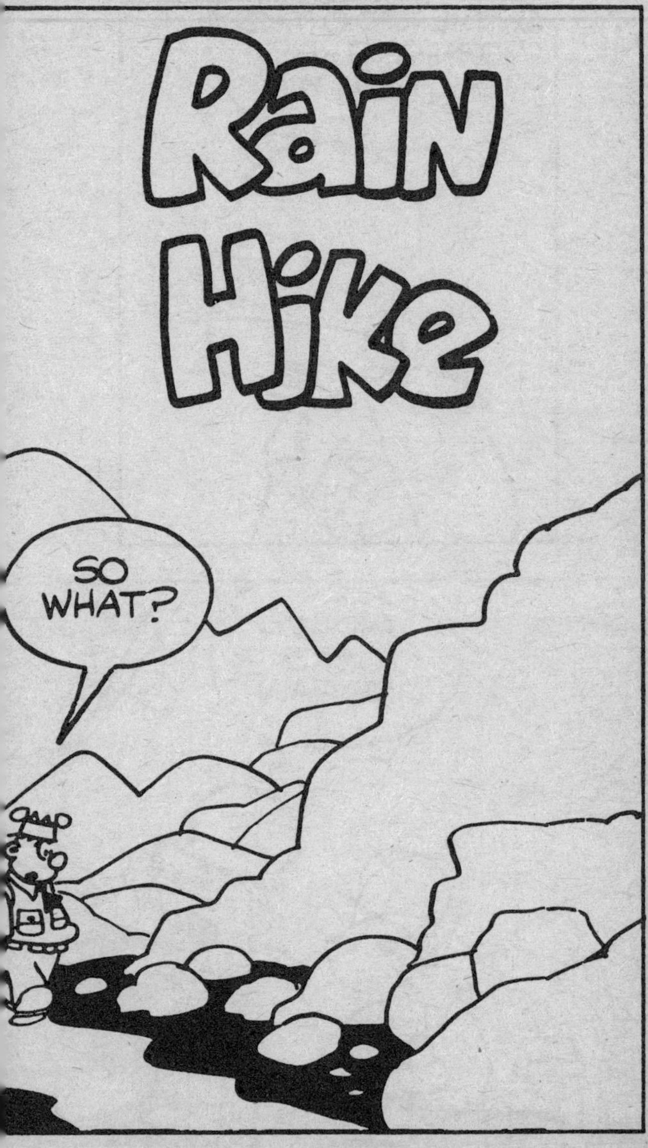
Rain Hike
SO WHAT?

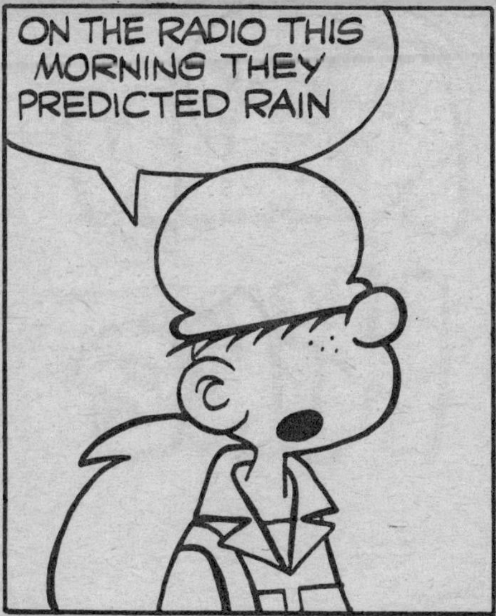
ON THE RADIO THIS MORNING THEY PREDICTED RAIN

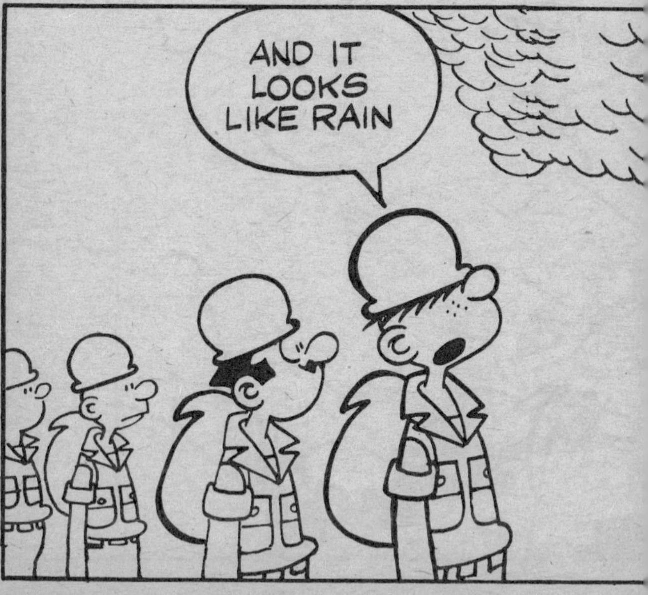
AND IT LOOKS LIKE RAIN

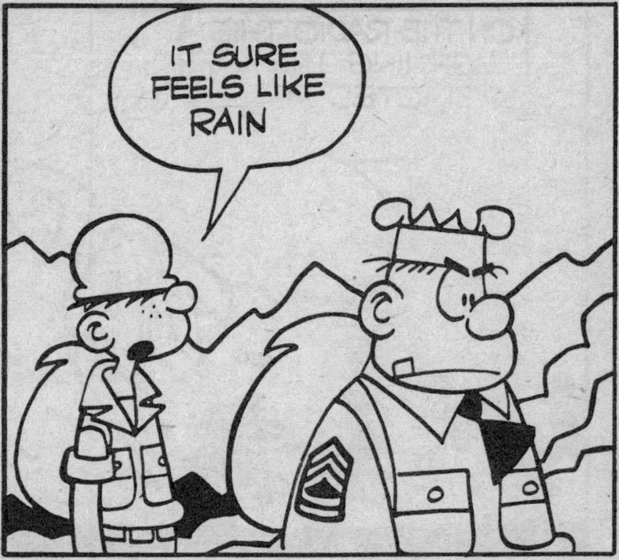
IT SURE FEELS LIKE RAIN

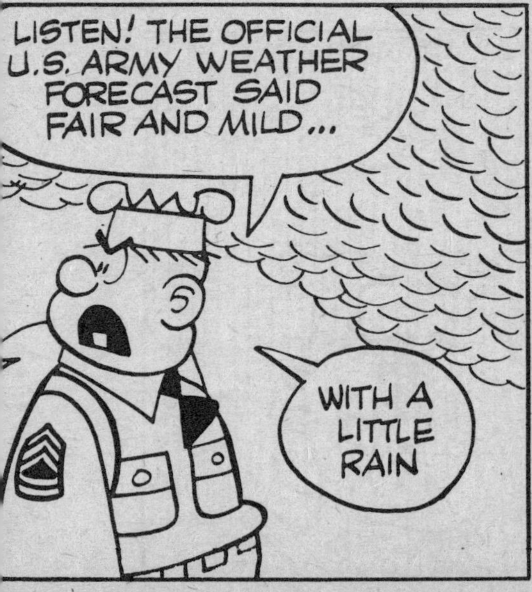
LISTEN! THE OFFICIAL U.S. ARMY WEATHER FORECAST SAID FAIR AND MILD...
WITH A LITTLE RAIN

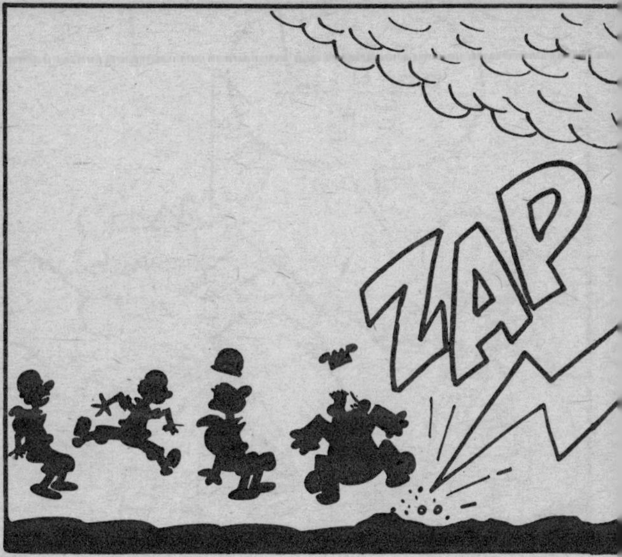
ZAP

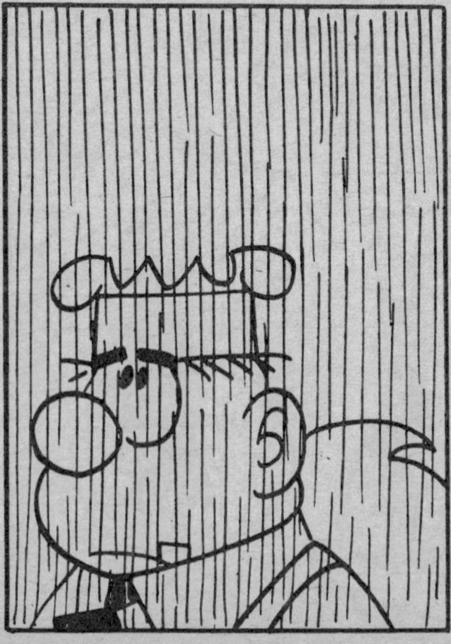

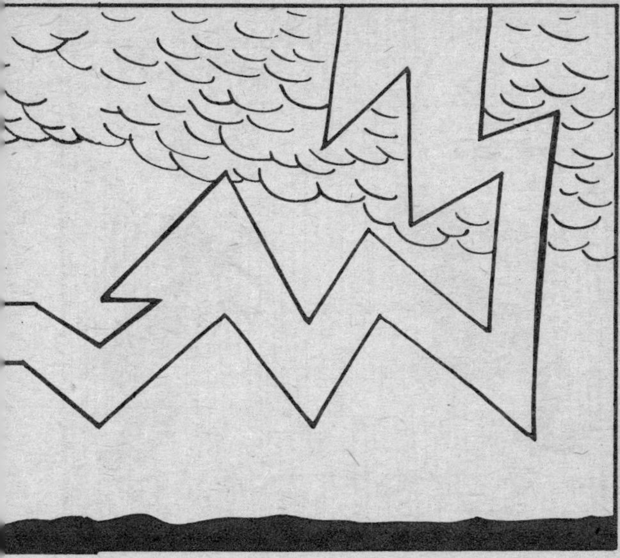

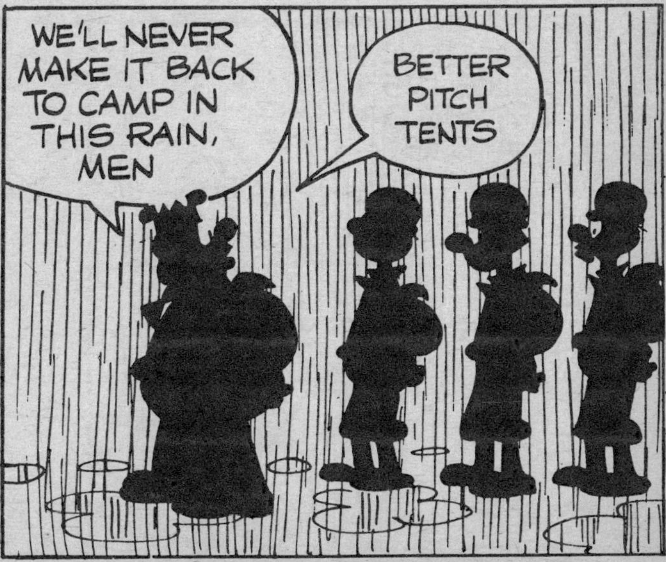
WE'LL NEVER MAKE IT BACK TO CAMP IN THIS RAIN, MEN
BETTER PITCH TENTS

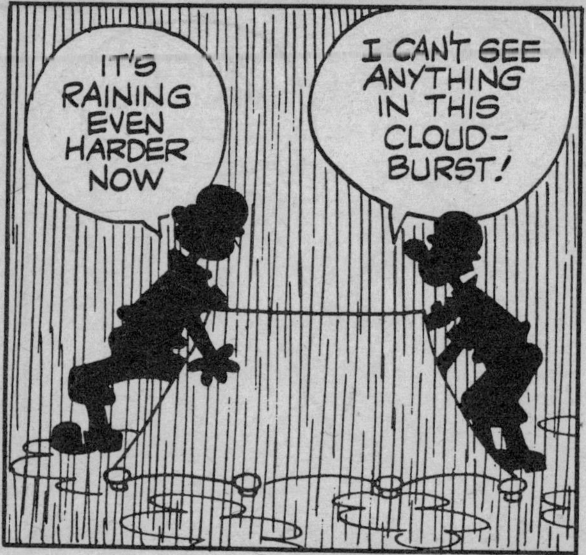
IT'S RAINING EVEN HARDER NOW
I CAN'T SEE ANYTHING IN THIS CLOUD-BURST!

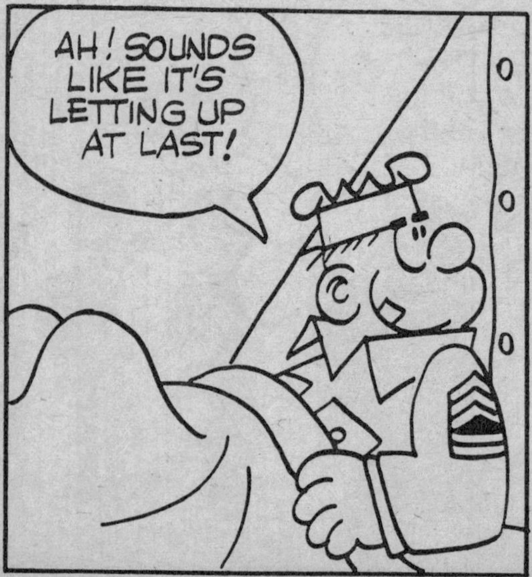
AH! SOUNDS LIKE IT'S LETTING UP AT LAST!

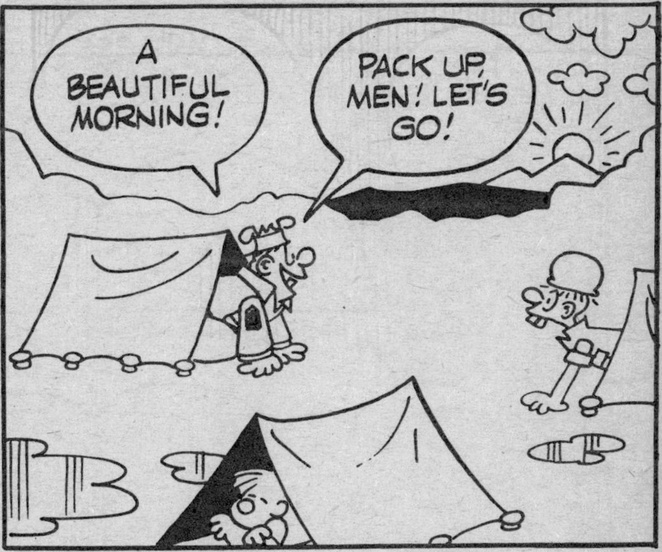
A BEAUTIFUL MORNING!
PACK UP, MEN! LET'S GO!

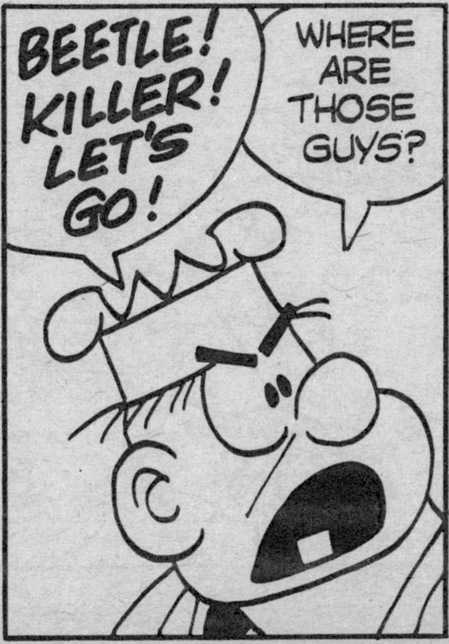
BEETLE! KILLER! LET'S GO!
WHERE ARE THOSE GUYS?

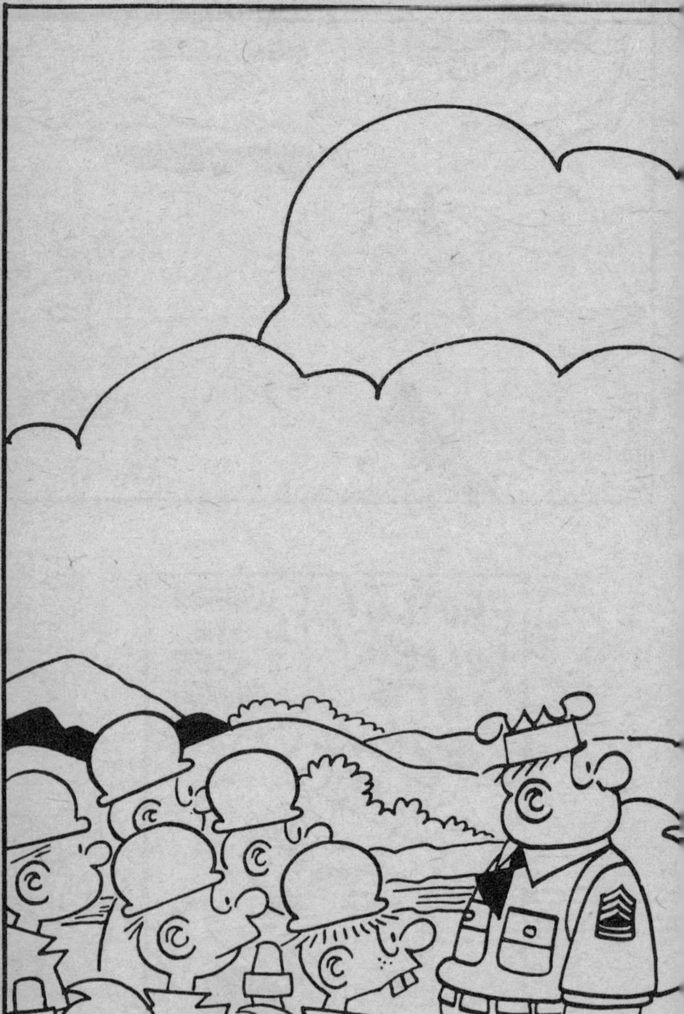

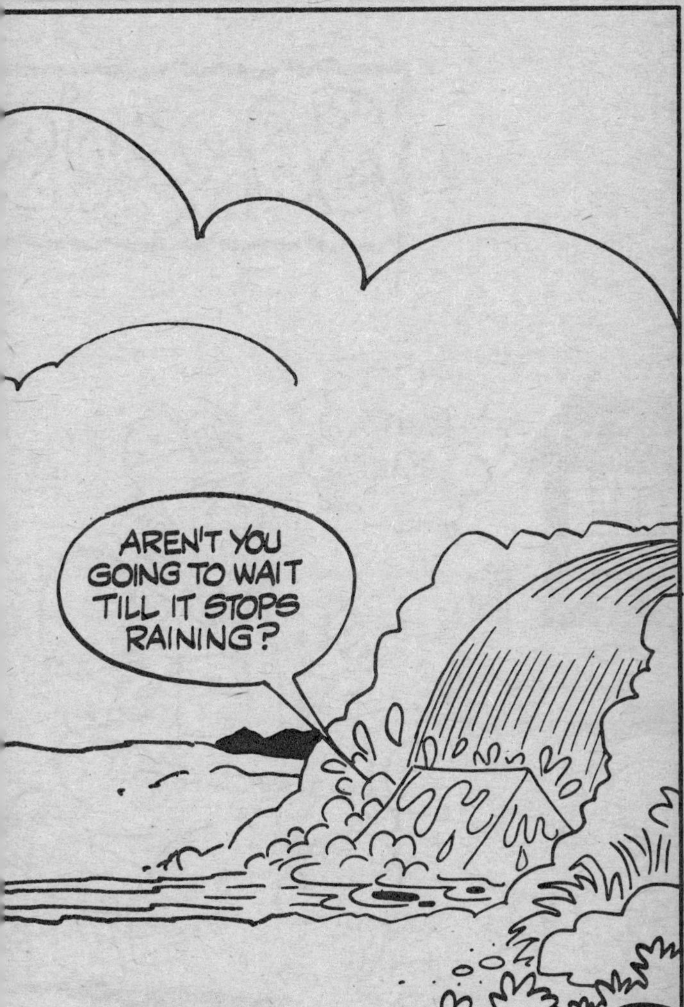
AREN'T YOU GOING TO WAIT TILL IT STOPS RAINING?
END

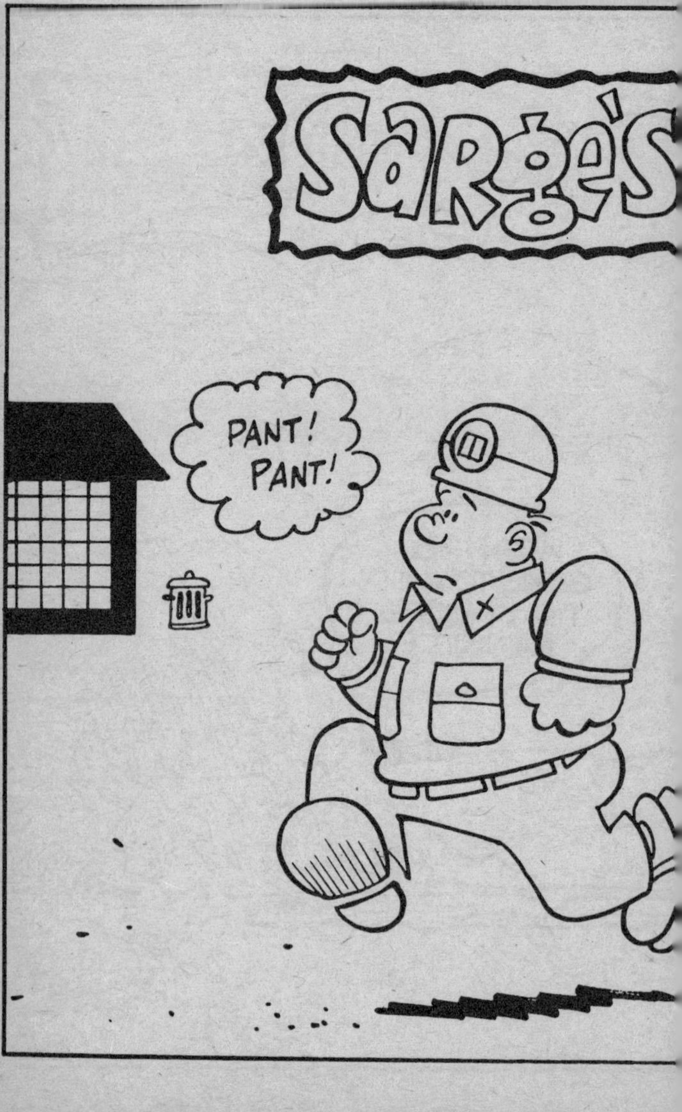
SARGE'S
PANT!
PANT!

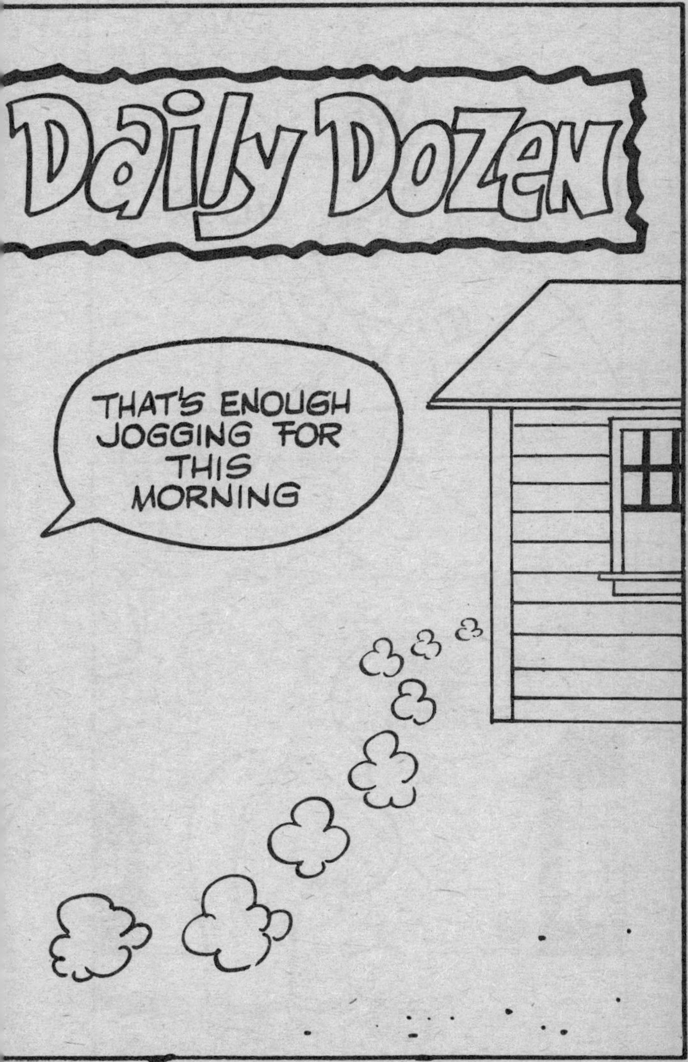
Daily Dozen
THAT'S ENOUGH JOGGING FOR THIS MORNING

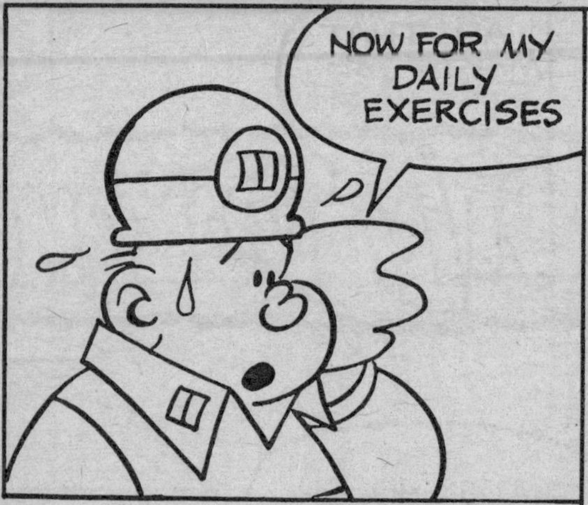
NOW FOR MY DAILY EXERCISES

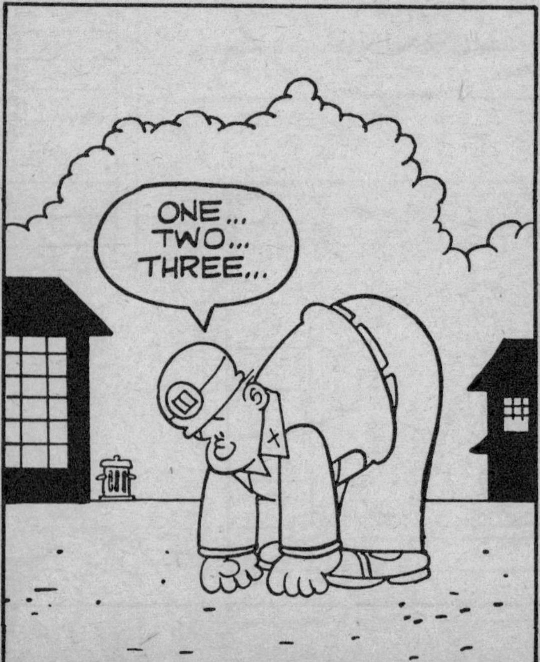
ONE... TWO... THREE...

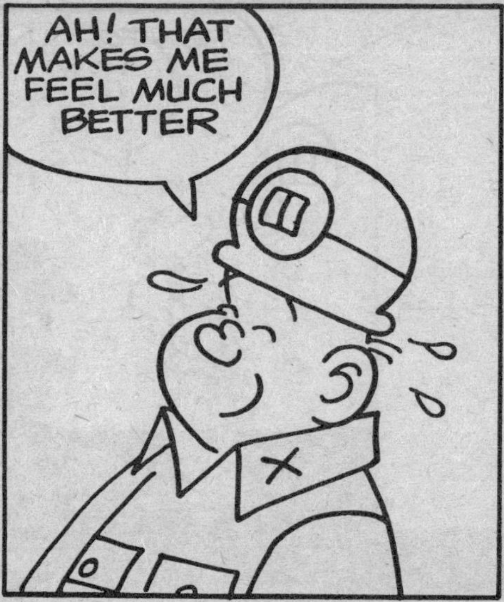
AH! THAT MAKES ME FEEL MUCH BETTER

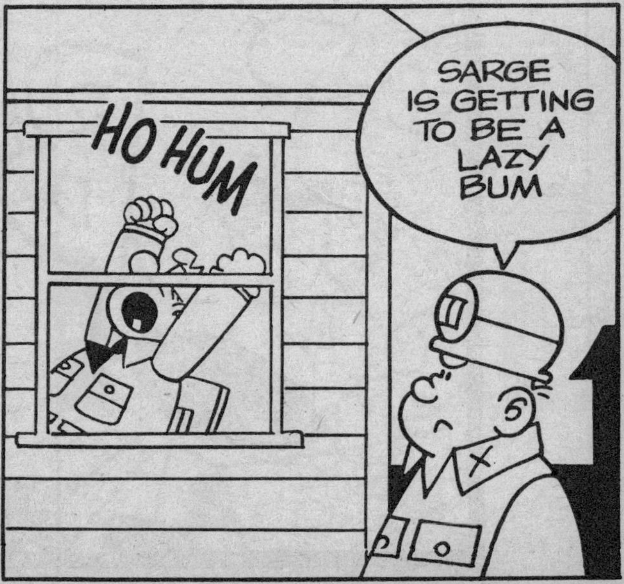
HO HUM
SARGE IS GETTING TO BE A LAZY BUM

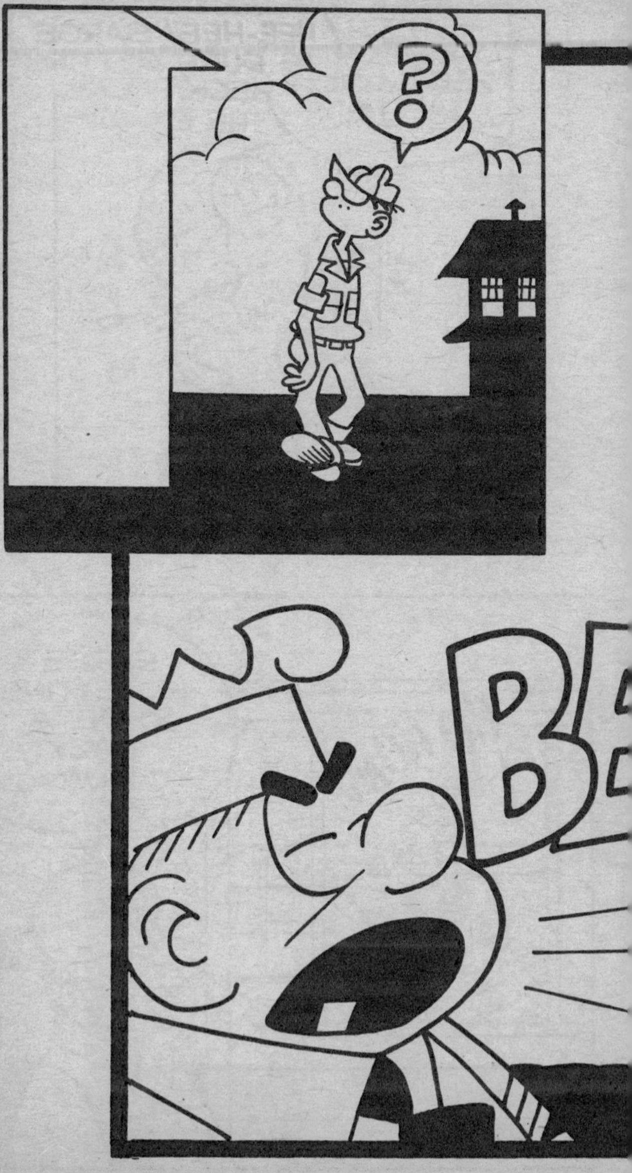
?

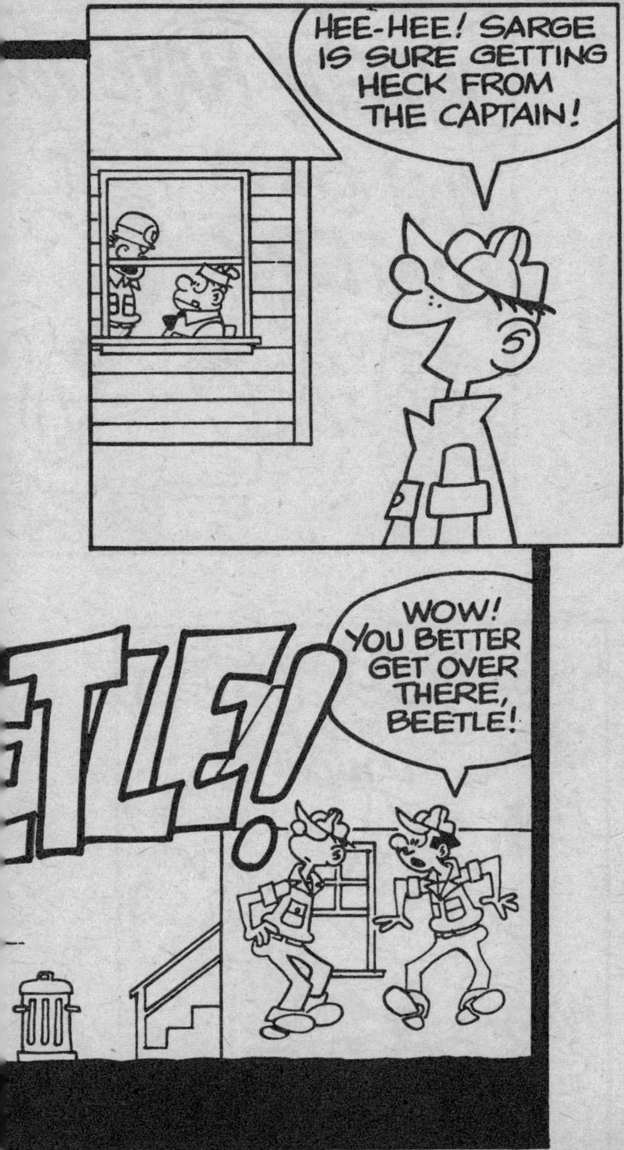
HEE-HEE! SARGE IS SURE GETTING HECK FROM THE CAPTAIN!
ETLE!
WOW! YOU BETTER GET OVER THERE, BEETLE!

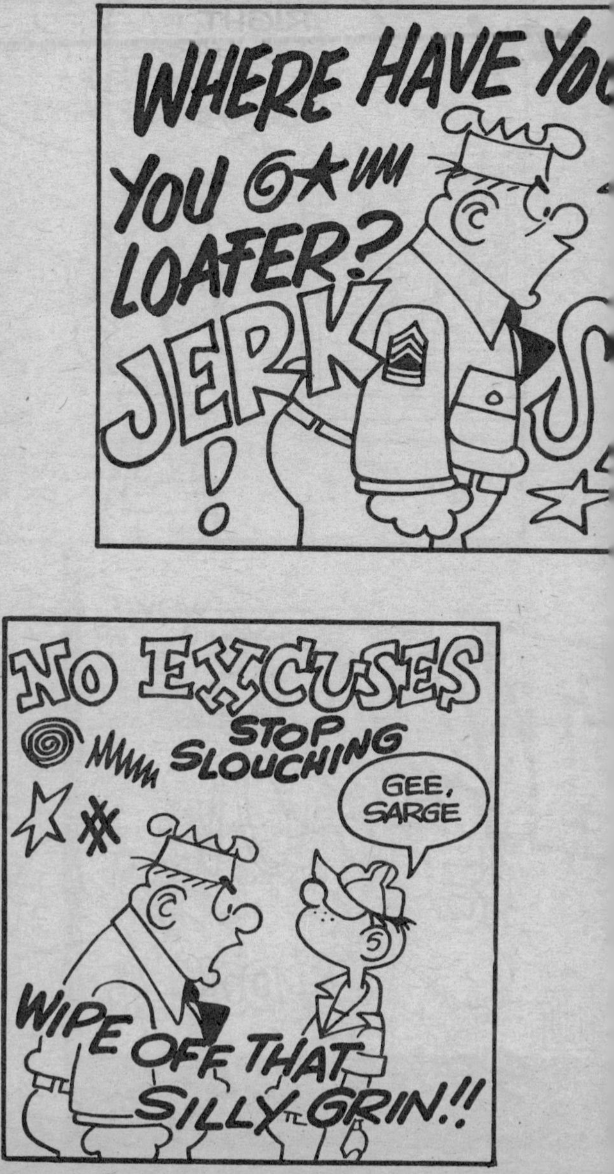
WHERE HAVE YO
YOU
LOAFER?
JERKS!
NO EXCUSES
STOP SLOUCHING
GEE, SARGE
WIPE OFF THAT SILLY GRIN!!

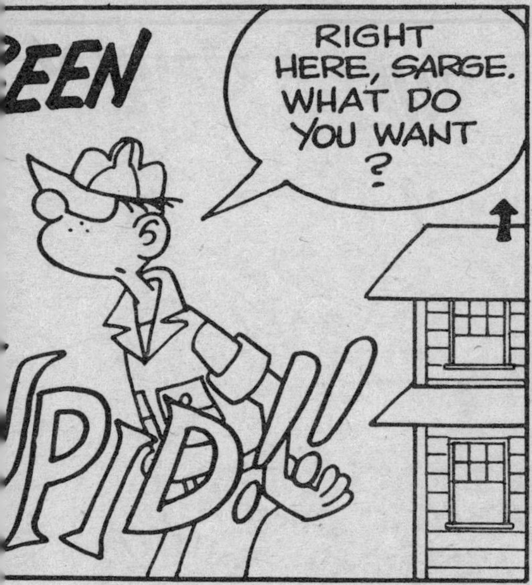
EEN
RIGHT HERE, SARGE. WHAT DO YOU WANT ?
PID!

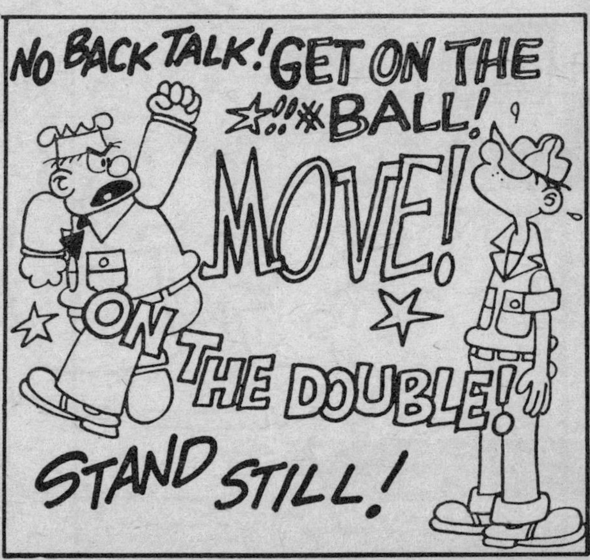
NO BACK TALK! GET ON THE
☆!!!*BALL!
MOVE!
ON THE DOUBLE!
STAND STILL!

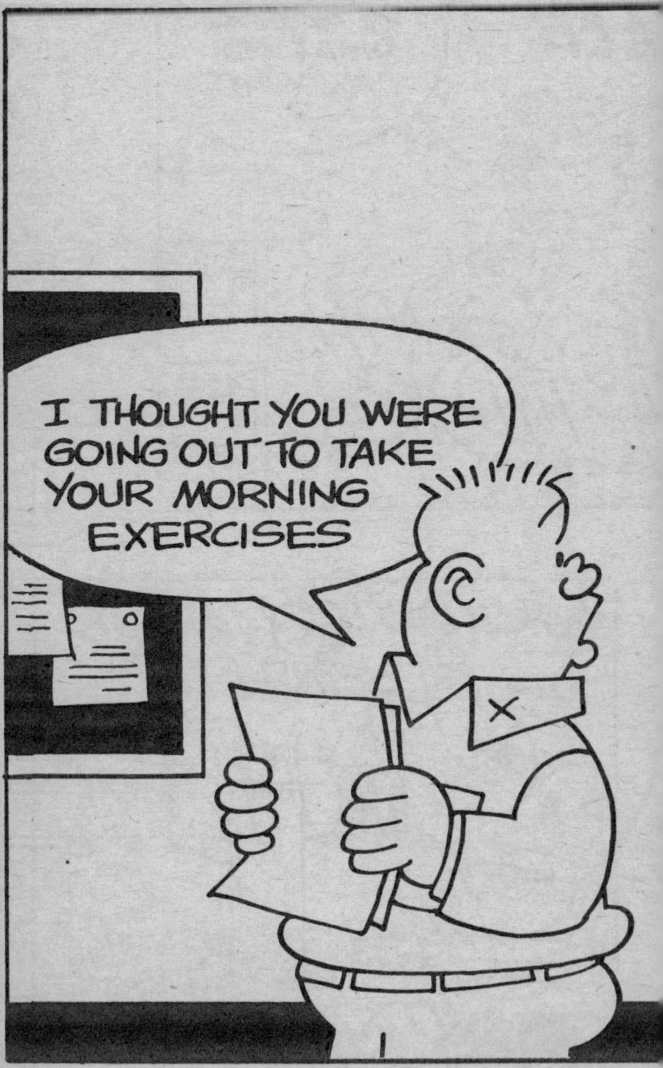
I THOUGHT YOU WERE GOING OUT TO TAKE YOUR MORNING EXERCISES

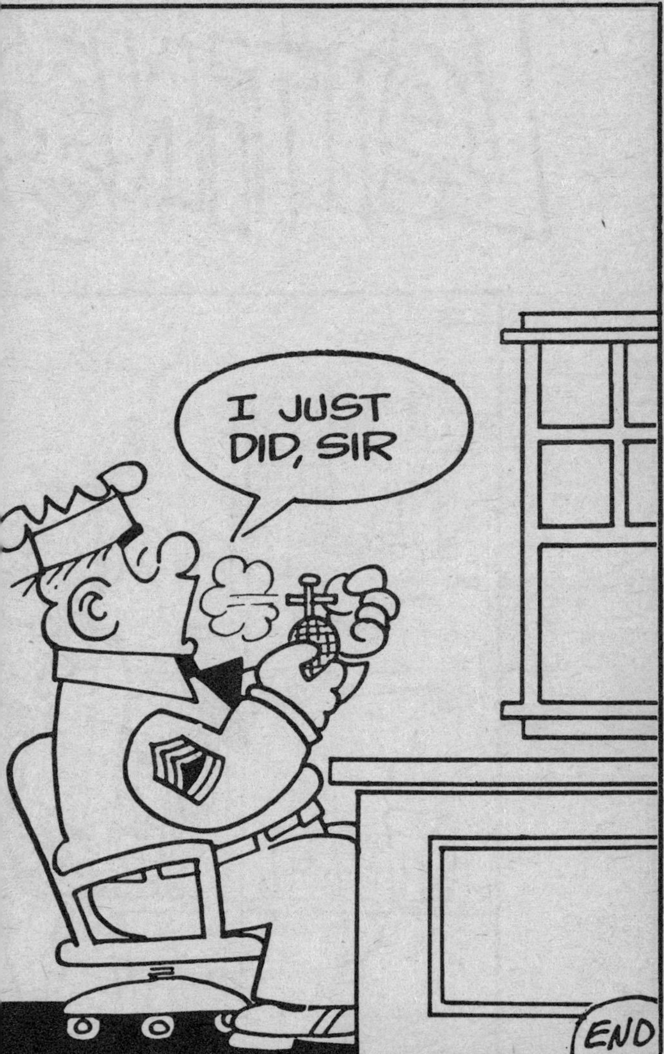
I JUST DID, SIR
END

LETTING

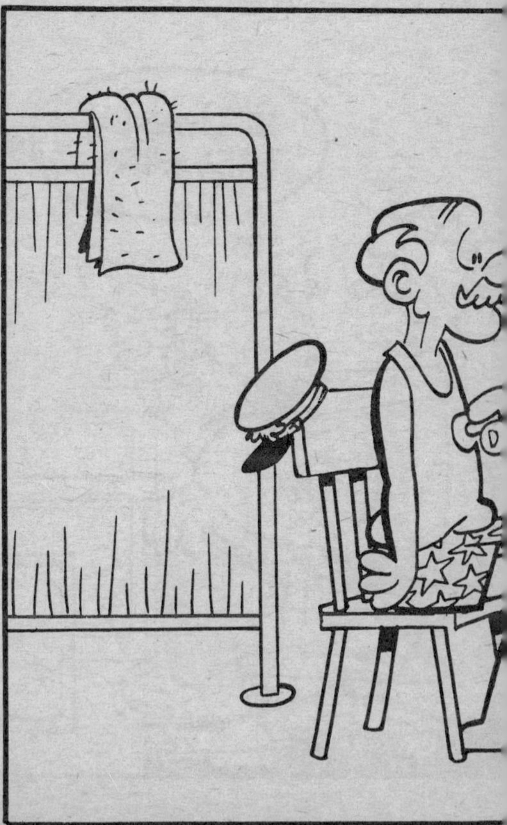

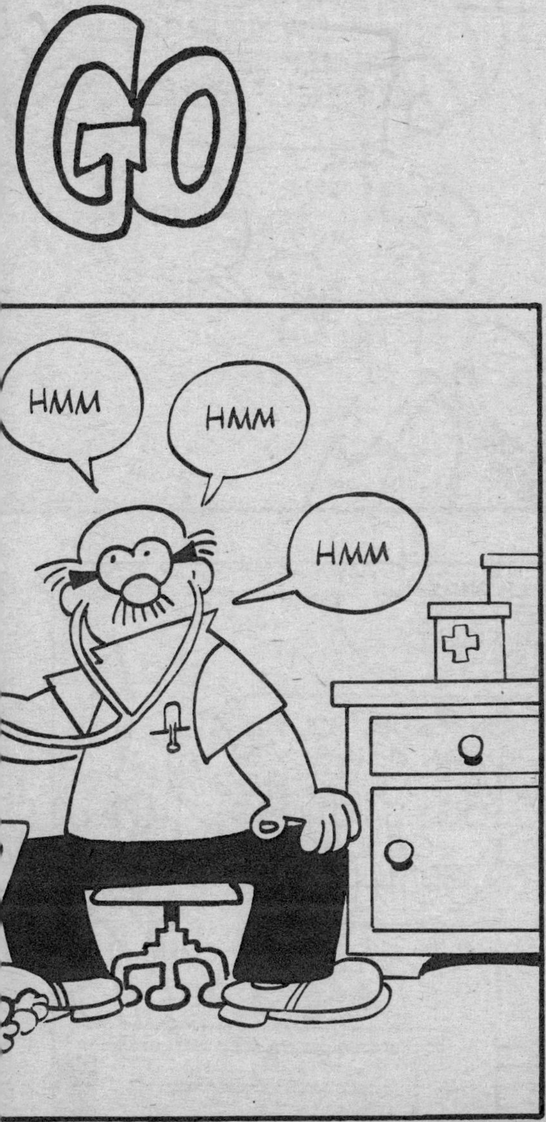
GO
HMM
HMM
HMM

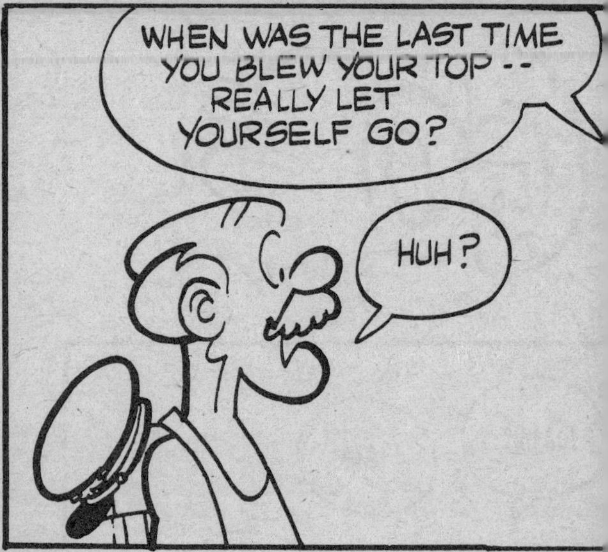
WHEN WAS THE LAST TIME YOU BLEW YOUR TOP -- REALLY LET YOURSELF GO?
HUH?

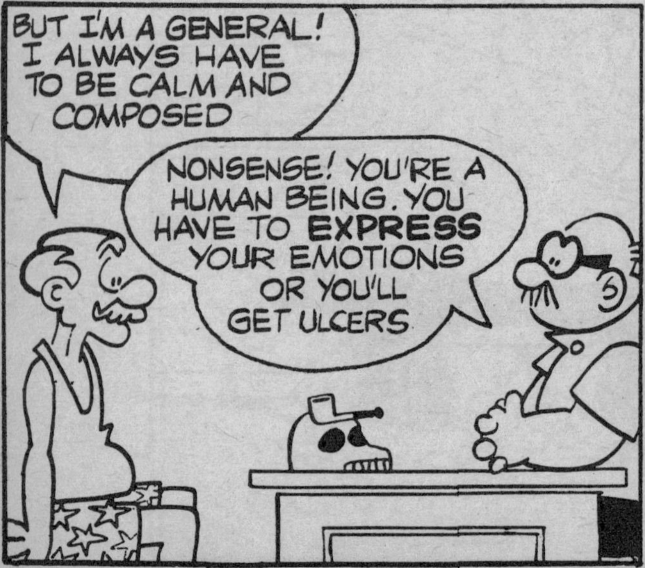
BUT I'M A GENERAL! I ALWAYS HAVE TO BE CALM AND COMPOSED
NONSENSE! YOU'RE A HUMAN BEING. YOU HAVE TO **EXPRESS** YOUR EMOTIONS OR YOU'LL GET ULCERS

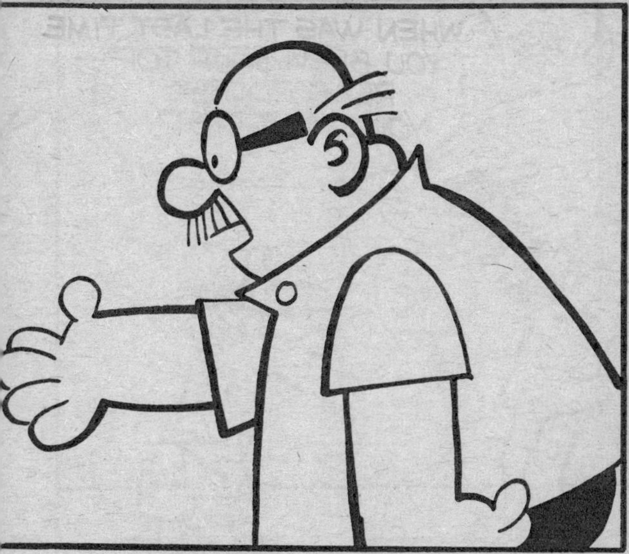

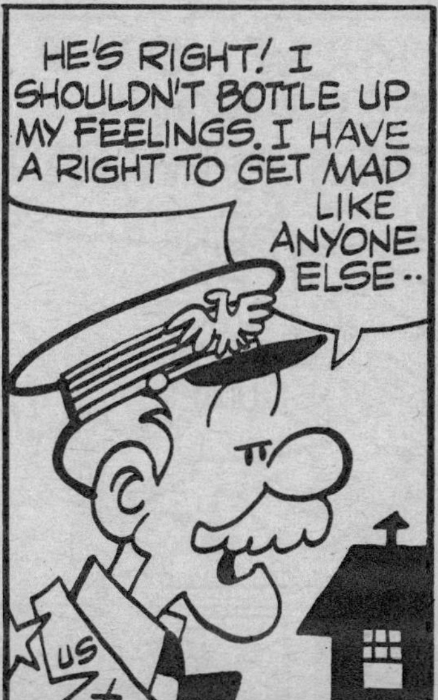
HE'S RIGHT! I SHOULDN'T BOTTLE UP MY FEELINGS. I HAVE A RIGHT TO GET MAD LIKE ANYONE ELSE..
US

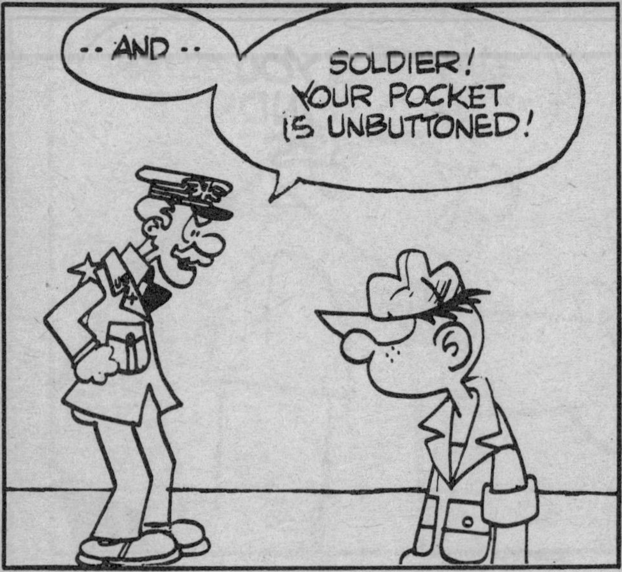
-- AND --
SOLDIER! YOUR POCKET IS UNBUTTONED!

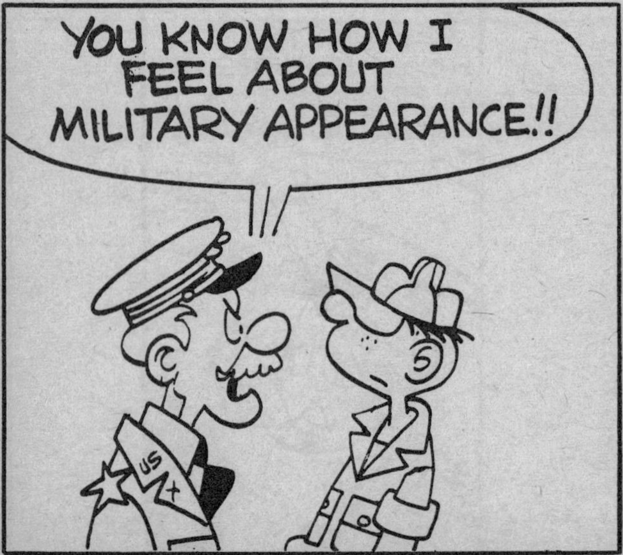
YOU KNOW HOW I FEEL ABOUT MILITARY APPEARANCE!!

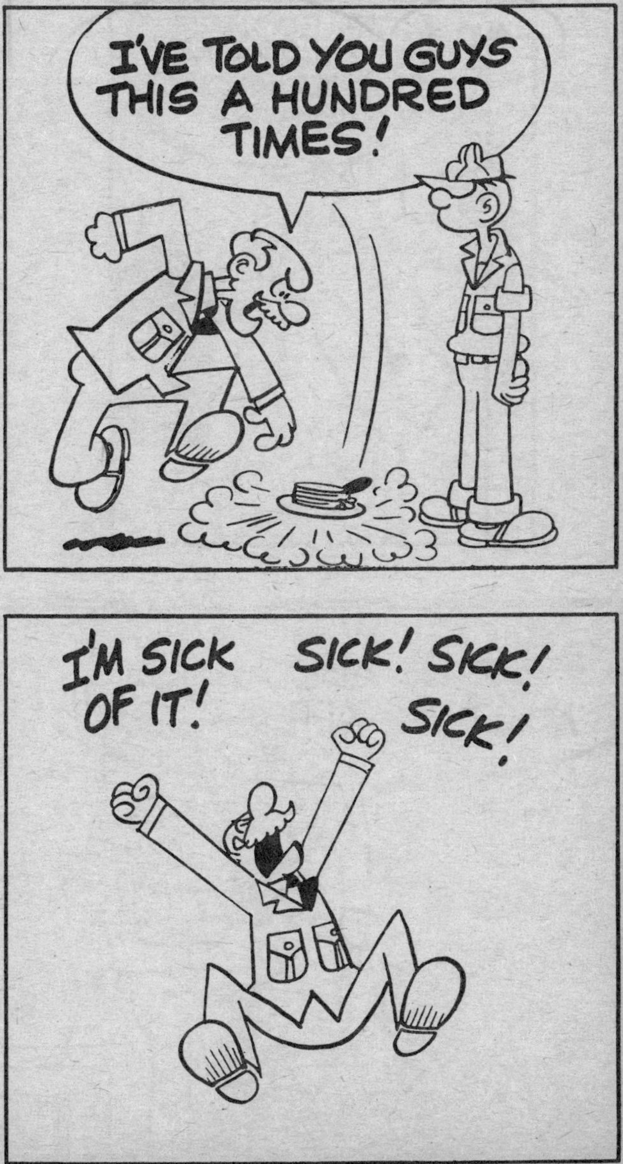
I'VE TOLD YOU GUYS THIS A HUNDRED TIMES!
I'M SICK OF IT!
SICK! SICK!
SICK!

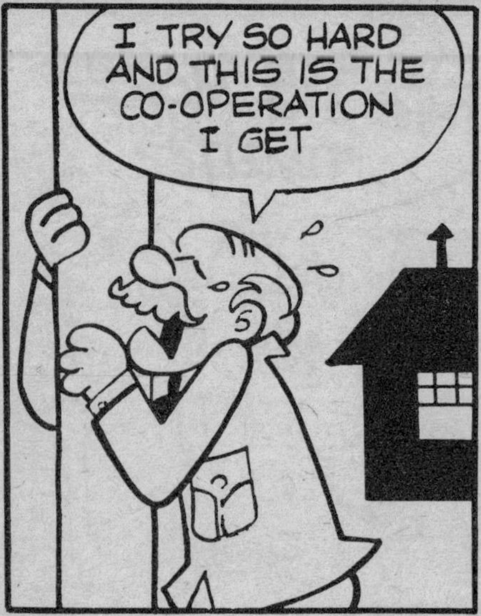
I TRY SO HARD AND THIS IS THE CO-OPERATION I GET

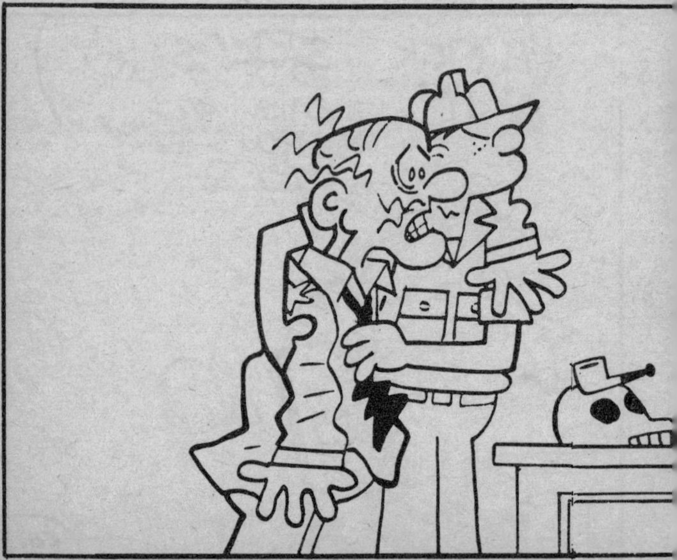

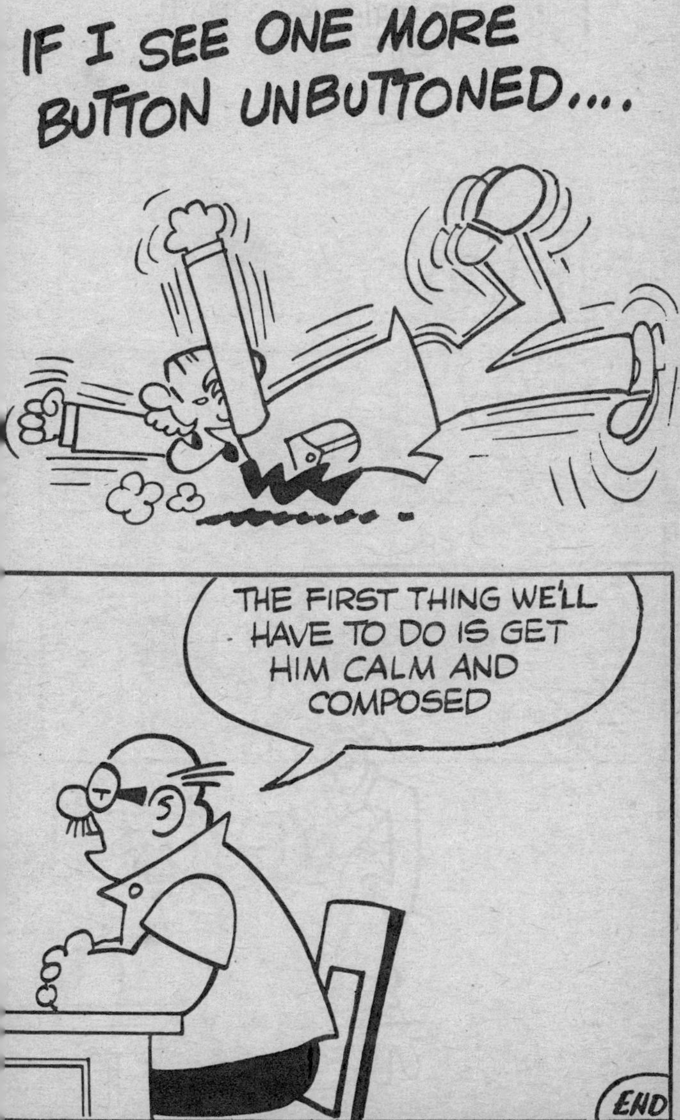
IF I SEE ONE MORE BUTTON UNBUTTONED....
THE FIRST THING WE'LL HAVE TO DO IS GET HIM CALM AND COMPOSED
END

the

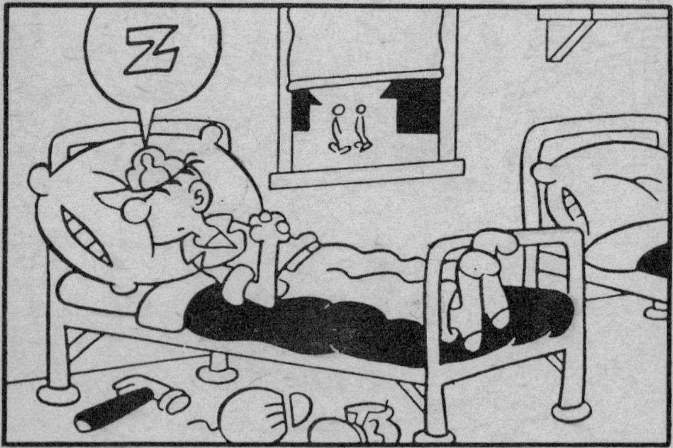
Z

end